SLUMMING

Also by

Kristen D. Randle

Breaking Rank
The Only Alien on the Planet

SLUMMING

Kristen D. Randle

HarperTempest
A Division of HarperCollinsPublishers

Slumming

Copyright © 2003 by Kristen D. Randle

All rights reserved. No part of this book may be used or
reproduced in any manner whatsoever without written permission
except in the case of brief quotations embodied in critical articles
and reviews. Printed in the United States of America.
For information address HarperCollins Children's Books,
a division of HarperCollins Publishers,
1350 Avenue of the Americas,
New York, NY 10019.
www.harpertempest.com

Library of Congress Cataloging-in-Publication Data

Randle, Kristen D.

Slumming / Kristen D. Randle.

p.   cm.

Summary: In their senior year of high school, three best friends,
Nikki, Alicia, and Sam, attempt an "experiment" in which they each
befriend a classmate they think needs attention and try to improve
that person's life.

ISBN 0-06-001022-3 — ISBN 0-06-001023-1 (lib. bdg.)

[1. Self-perception—Fiction. 2. Interpersonal relations—Fiction.
3. Family problems—Fiction. 4. Mormons—Fiction. 5. Best
friends—Fiction. 6. Friendship—Fiction. 7. High Schools—Fiction.
8. Schools—Fiction.] 1. Title.

PZ7.R1585 Sl 2003

[Fic]—dc21   2002032812

Typography by Lizzy Bromley

7 8 9 10

❖

First Edition

For
Jen Hyde,
who helped each of my kids
navigate through high school and
won their love and respect

And for Guy,
the good father

ACKNOWLEDGMENTS

You don't have to read this. Really—you can just go ahead and start the story. I simply wanted a chance to thank some of the people (often mistakenly categorized as adults) who have been true and faithful friends to my kids. These guys just keep ending up in my books, one way or another. This page is just me, writing in some of their yearbooks at the end of the day:

FRIENDS - 4 - EVER

Jen Hyde	Mike Carson	Shawna Hatch
Dennis Pratt	The Randles	Geneva Feland
Merrill Webb	The Morrises	Lakeside 6th
Alan Ashton	Orren Crow	Linda Worsley
Mr. Edwards	The Jensens	Mrs. Drussel
Ron Harris	Donny Bills	Jeannie Biggs
Jim Darrington	Kathy Busker	The Brands
Rachel Rubow	The Rowlands	Mr. Denfeld
The Hoffmans	Ms. Cooper	Yankee Clipper
The McLeans	Ms. Werner	Mike Hollister
Jana Jenson	The Beesons	Gigi and Jim
The Butterfields	The Perrys	Jeanette King
Ray Smith	Tonya Barkdull	Mrs. Teeter
Monica and Steve Call	Sharon Shinn	The Kews
The Downeys	Rosemary Brosnan	The Cards
Kelly Wallis	The Mannings	O. Hatch
LaRene Braithwaite	Janice Dennis	The Parkins
Georgia Connally	Keven Crawford	Ginger Lewis
Tim Gee	Mike Downey	The Castors
The Shaws	Ms. Griffin	Aunt Donna
Lois Dettenmaier	Ms. Hook	

And all the other dear ones

#1

Nikki

There's something about traveling to another country: you can never see your own home quite the same way again. I believe it was this experience that inspired my Great Philosophical Idea. Not that I am necessarily blaming the French. Or my mother.

French faces don't look like American faces. It's hard to explain. "Not a physical difference," my mother told me, "so much as a philosophical one." We were leaning on the stone rampart along the Seine, watching five young musicians arguing with a couple of Paris policemen. "The French fit themselves into the universe in a different way than we do." My mother grinned and shrugged, looking a bit French herself. "The spirit inside shapes the face."

I remembered those words one day as I was watching Brian Camarga walk across the school lunchroom. And *voilà*—the Great Idea.

Of course, the second it came into my head, I started talking about it. This is one of my character flaws. Then Alicia jumped on the idea, sucked it in, remodeled it, and out it came: a new edition of Alicia's Perky Projects. This is one of *her* character flaws.

And suddenly, Sam and I were trapped.

Anyway, that's how it all got started. So *mea culpa*— everything that happened later can be traced straight back to me. Big surprise.

Brian Camarga is a classic nerd. He's tall and skinny, has lousy skin, wears glasses, and carries about fifty mechanical pencils in his shirt pocket. He dresses like an old man, he has terrible posture, and he gets straight A's. He is, in short, a walking stereotype.

As it happens, I also get straight A's. But I am none of the above things. In fact, I am reasonably cute, I have tons of friends, pretty good hair, and I am friendly to everybody. I'm not your student government type like Alicia is. I'm just a happy person who generally likes going to school. My flaws are that I talk too much, and I have a problem with low self-esteem.

Sam

"Nikki talks too much." I say this to Alicia—not because I am annoyed. I say it because it is true.

"She talks a lot because she has a lot to say," Alicia retorts. "You know, Sam, it wouldn't hurt some people to do a little *more* talking."

"Oh, and you're the one to say that," I remark.

"All right," she admits. "It might not hurt either of us."

I am not concerned. "I have a Jeep," I tell her. "I don't have to talk."

Nikki

Not everybody likes me. Some people see me from the outside and conclude that I'm obnoxious and fake and shallow. Too bad they don't look closer.

Which brings me to the point: there are all kinds of people in the world. Tolstoy once said, "All happy people are the same; but unhappy people are all interesting." Those aren't the exact words, but that's the gist of it, and personally, I think it's trash. Happy people, unhappy people—everybody is interesting. And nobody's the same.

It's sad that some people's lives end up being so depressingly unhappy. A person raised in a messed-up family can be cursed with a seriously skewed view of himself and the world. On the other hand, a person raised in a great family can get a solid head start into a good life.

Or not. Sometimes it's just the opposite. Life is complex.

But that's the game, isn't it? Who you turn out to be in the end. What kind of hand they deal you, and how you choose to play it. Or at least, that's the way it seems to me.

So I was looking at Brian, and I wondered—obviously, smart people do not have to be so completely repulsive. And then I thought, French faces, American faces—what makes the difference? Everybody has two eyes and a nose and a mouth. What makes some people beautiful and some people not?

Alicia

I will admit that when we read *Pygmalion* in junior English, it made a deep impression on me. And when Nikki started talking about French faces and about Brian, I knew exactly what she meant. Even if everybody in the world had exactly the same face, there would be no two people exactly alike. Some would achieve beauty, some would be ugly; some faces would end up seeming gentle, some cruel. All depending on the person looking out through the face.

For a long time, I've wanted to find out if this is actually true. And suddenly, today, I realized: we're seniors. This is the end—we graduate in less than two months. So if I ever want to do something big, something that has meaning, it better be now.

The idea came all at once: we will each choose a person who is obviously untapped, and we will try to open him up, set him free, give him life. I do not anticipate that it will be that hard—kindness, a little attention, support, friendship.

I want to work a miracle.

I set the rules: we have three weeks. We will choose our person, do whatever it takes, and then we will take the person we have chosen to the prom. The day after the prom, the three of us will get together and decide who accomplished the biggest change. That last part is the part I like least— the competition, I mean—but I felt I had to make it that way because some people work better under pressure.

I have to defend it like this: the three of us have a lot

to give. It would be a crime if, before we leave this part of our lives forever, we don't do something to make the world better for somebody. Somebody who may be drowning. Somebody whose heart is dying.

Somebody like Morgan.

Sam

It was a stupid idea.

I have a term paper. I have a life. I should have said no. But I hate arguing.

Alicia says, "Choose a target with potential." And I do. Then Nikki blows up in my face.

"Why her?" Nikki yells. Like I broke the rules.

But I didn't. My target is smart and interesting. I think that counts as potential.

She's just so completely not me.

Nikki

We have AP's and finals and term papers; it's not like we need another project. But I let this get away from me.

Maybe the idea of changing Brian was so intriguing, I just lost my head. Anyway, here we go: a human experiment.

I walked away with two main misgivings. First, three weeks is not a long time to turn somebody like Brian around. For sure, you can't clear up skin that fast—but then, that's just a minor detail. The big thing is going to be his self-confidence. Fix that, and stuff like posture, taste in clothes—all that will just naturally follow.

The real worry here is that Alicia won't tell us who she's choosing. I'm betting she picked Peter—it's just her pride that won't let her admit it. He's the natural choice, darned good material to begin with. But you never can tell with Alicia—especially considering what she's been going through lately.

But Sam. Why would he choose *Tia*? Tia Terraletto: Girl Most Likely to Beat You with Chains. When she walks by, boys die instantly of asphyxiation. I spoke to her once, and she reduced me to ashes. She scares me to death. Here's my question: why would *she* just pop into Samuel Pittman's head?

Alicia

Nikki's going to rag me all weekend. But telling was

never in the rules. Besides, I heard the way she went after Sam when he picked Tia.

I don't think my dad needs to know about this little project. He has too much to worry about as it is. Anyway, it's not that big a thing. Just me trying to make a difference.

Sam

There's a reason why people wear black lipstick. The eyebrow ring, the Nazi shoes—that whole hard-guy thing—it means something. Says something. Like "up yours." Okay, so it's an attitude. You're rejecting what's normal.

But why? Why bother?

I like people. I like liking stuff—football and assemblies and knowing everybody I pass in the hall. And singing. And church. And believing in things.

Not rejection. I don't like that—rejecting. Or being rejected.

Tia's a good artist. That's what Mr. Russo says. She was in his exhibit last year. I didn't understand her drawings. They made me feel weird—I had to go look at trees and grass afterward. Normal things. Simple things.

I think she's unhappy.

Maybe I could do something about that.

Nikki

I told my mom about the Brian Camarga Epiphany. I didn't tell her about the prom. I'm not sure how I feel about that yet. But I'm kind of excited about helping Brian. I thought Mom would get it, but she didn't. Even when I brought up French faces.

"Everybody has to be American?" she asked me. I told her that wasn't the point. It's not that I want Brian to be like *me*. I explained very cogently: there's a lot of untapped potential in Brian that could be brought out if he were maybe a little bit more self-confident.

When I said that, my mother started getting sarcastic. So I just let it go. It doesn't pay to get into a debate with my mother.

Anyway, Monday is when we will begin our Human Project. No worries. Piece of cake—once I can figure out how to break into the myopic world of Brian Camarga.

#2

Nikki

This is not going to be easy.

I had the perfect opening: Mr. Webb assigned the term project in zoology today. We already knew he was going to pair us up for this; the fact that he was assigning partners today and letting us choose our own—it seemed like destiny.

Luckily, he started at the top of the roll. "Ainsworth," he called, not even looking up, "who's your partner?" Since my name happens to start with *B*—one of the few perks to having a name like Bickerstaff—I got to name pretty much anybody I wanted.

I know Peter expected me to name him. We sit at the same table and we work well together—besides which, he'd already told me his idea about sampling native grasshopper populations. Not to mention the fact that he and I have compatible GPA's and he is so darned cute.

But I wanted Brian Camarga.

While Mr. Webb duly noted our odd partnership, people sitting around me smirked. So what? I was ecstatic. I turned to grin at Brian—you know, give him a little "Hi, partner" wave.

I'm going to be honest here. I'm not that used to having people reject me. Okay, maybe I'm not a big favorite of people like Tia Terraletto. But I don't think it was such a stretch of the imagination on my part, expecting Brian Camarga to be surprised and pleased that I had chosen him.

Except that I was completely and absolutely wrong.

When I gave him that little wave, all cute and ready to bestow on him the glory of my partnership, I was surprised to see that he appeared to be glaring at me. I mean, it's hard to tell exactly what's going on behind those fishbowl glasses of his. But he definitely did not look happy.

I thought maybe he didn't realize that I was looking at him. After all, it's a long way from the back of the room to the front for somebody with weak eyes. So I kicked up the volume on my friendly smile, and I pointed at him. This did not get any change in response at all.

Mr. Webb gave us the rest of the period to work on our concept, which meant that we were supposed to sit together. In our teams.

I waited a minute, giving Brian a chance to get his books together and move up to my table. But when I looked back there again, he hadn't moved. He was still staring. In fact, his mouth was hanging open.

Okay.

I picked up my stuff, and I went all the way back to his table. I put my books down. After that, I had to trudge once more to the front of the room to get my chair.

"You want me to carry that for you?" Peter asked.

But he was not the one who should have offered. I thanked him graciously, then picked up the chair and lugged it, single-handedly, all the way back again to Brian Camarga's table.

I sat down in my chair, I folded my arms, and I looked at him. He still hadn't moved. "Well," I said.

He hadn't even closed his mouth.

"I'm Nikki," I said, in case he still couldn't see me clearly.

"Why did you do this?" he asked. His voice is kind of nasal.

"I thought you would make an excellent partner," I said encouragingly.

"I can't believe you did this," he said, still staring at me.

I nodded. "Yeah," I said. "Well. So what do you think we ought to work on?"

He raised both hands up in front of his face, almost like he was going to pray. He has very long fingers. "Calvin and I were going to be partners," he said, doing these little chopping things with his hands for emphasis. "Calvin and I decided to work on this project *weeks* ago."

"So now it's you and me," I said brightly.

He pushed both hands onto his forehead. "You just don't get it," he said. "This was supposed to be Calvin's and my project. You have *stolen* Calvin's place. You have *stolen* my grade in this class. I need a *partner.* Calvin is supposed to be my *partner.* My working *partner.* They could still change their minds at MIT, you know. They still want to see my last semester transcript. I do not understand why you did this."

Now I was staring at him.

"Maybe I needed a good partner myself," I pointed out.

"Well, *that's* obvious," he said, smirking.

"What's that supposed to mean?" I asked him, heating up.

He rolled his eyes. "Now, how'm I gonna get any kind of grade in this class?" he muttered.

"Just a minute, here, sonny," I said, sounding a lot like my mom. "What you're saying is—you think I'm going to hold you back?"

He gave me that dumb mouth-hanging-open look again. "You're brighter than I thought," he said.

"You got me," I confided. "My plan was to hook up with somebody really smart so I could get a free ride. Maybe bring my GPA up to a point five. Maybe even work on my *grooming* skills while you're doing the research."

"I need Calvin," he moaned faintly.

"Fine," I said, and I looked around for Calvin Sweeney. Nothing was worth this. My intention was to switch partners. Until I saw who Calvin had gotten stuck with. There are limits to what I will do, even in the name of humanitarian service. After all, I needed a grade in this class.

"Would it interest you to know," I said, leaning forward till I was right in Brian Camarga's face, "that my GPA is hovering right now between a 3.99 and a 4.15?" My AP scores were all up in the five range, which explains the extra fifteen hundredth.

That close, his eyes looked like watery, mutant goldfish. He blinked them. "Huh-uh," he said, narrowing his eyes.

"Uh-huh," I said. "And I don't appreciate it that you made the assumption otherwise simply on the basis of my gender, thank you."

He blinked again. "It's not your gender," he said.

"Then what is it?" I asked, with dangerously sweet patience.

He closed his mouth. "I don't want to talk about this," he said. "What did you get in Marston's class?"

"An A," I said.

"That's not bad," he said, beginning to go vague on me. "Well. Okay, then. Maybe we've got a chance. But I don't know. Calvin and I tailored this project to our team strengths. We work together really well. We play Majik by teams, and we *always* win."

"Well, you've got me there," I admitted. "I promise you won't ever have to play Majik with me. Why don't you tell me about the plans you had for the project?"

"What were *you* going to do?" he countered.

"Well, I hadn't really—"

"See?" He moaned, throwing his hands up in the air. "Calvin and I have been talking about this for *weeks*."

"It's not as if I don't have any ideas of my own," I said indignantly. "I was thinking about doing something based on the human genome—"

"No," he said. "We're doing messenger RNA."

"Swell," I said. "I'm fascinated by messenger RNA." Which only happens to be the truth.

"Then describe it to me," he said. "I'm not just talking about function here," he warned. "I want structures. Specific structures."

This is *not* going to be easy.

Sam

Why didn't I say no? Right at the beginning. I could have said no, and none of this would have happened. But I didn't. How stupid is that?

You know what makes me mad? It's when people who don't know me assume they've got me down. I get that "You think you're so cool" thing all the time. Why? I don't feel like that. I'm miles from feeling like that.

It's because of football, for one. Because I'm good at it. And because I get good grades. I enjoy football—but playing well was important because I needed the scholarship. That's why I tried so hard. Nobody ever watched me and said, "You know—you're a genius. Let us give you whatever you want." But people are always looking at me like, *You get everything for free.* None of this is magic; none of this has been easy for me.

When she looked at me this afternoon—I don't know.

I'm standing there by her locker, practically alone in the hall after school. She finally comes. I just say "Hi." And she gives me that *uh-huh* look. So okay, it was obvious I was waiting for her. I felt so stupid.

"I'm Sam Pittman," I say. And I smile. And still, she's just looking at me: *So what do you want?*

"Um . . ." That's all I can say. And then we're just staring.

Her lips are always black, since about two years ago. Black around the outside, like an outline, maroon in the middle. I have this vision of her very calmly doing that to herself, carefully drawing those lines on her lips.

"O—kay," she says. It comes out, *I'll play along with this for about two seconds.* She opens her locker.

"I just thought," I say, "I could get to know you."

She laughs. She doesn't even look up. She leans over, pulling books off the floor of her locker. I'm looking down at her head. Her hair stands up in a thousand little spikes, like some kind of—not a porcupine, more like a hedgehog. Then she straightens up. She gives me that same look my mother gets when she thinks I'm pulling something on her.

"Forget it," she says.

I am confused.

"What?" I say. "Forget what?"

"What you came sniffing around here for," she says. She slams her locker and starts walking down the hall. Just like that—just walks away.

"I'm not sniffing for anything," I say angrily, following, like she's pulling me down the hall after her. "I just thought—"

"And I told you," she says, spinning around. She does this thing with her eyes, like she's shooting sparks. "You can forget it."

Then she's gone.

And I am alone in the hall with my face burning.

Alicia

I like to sit by my window at night. I sit there and look out over the houses, out to where the moon hangs, so cold and clear in the dark. The moon is huge. Bigger than my house. Bigger than this city. Huge and far away, floating in nothing. When you see it that way, the things that happen to little individual people don't seem so big.

I had a test today in zoology, and I did really well. I have a gift for memorization, and that helps when you have to come up with phylums and families of things. I understand classification. I can recognize samples when they're sitting in jars.

That's the easy part—telling one simple life-form from another. All you have to do is identify the defining characteristics. I like doing it. You're either right or wrong. I enjoy having a chance to feel like I know something for sure.

I tried to talk to Sammy tonight, but he nearly bit my head off. So now I'm feeling restless. I don't know why he's mad at me. Unless it's because I won't tell them who my Pygmalion choice is. But some things are meant to be held close. Some things shrivel and die in the light of day.

I should probably be going to bed, but I don't want to. I don't fall asleep too well anymore. I like sitting by the window. Night is slow and silent. I look out at the moon and I wonder what my mother is doing tonight— if maybe she's looking up at the moon, wondering what we are doing.

#3

Sam

I want to say something.

This has to be very clear: I believe in God. This is true. It is my honest belief. And I believe that Christ is more than just a religious story; I believe he was a real person who walked on the earth two thousand years ago, and that somehow, after they crucified him, he came alive again, and by doing that, changed everything.

It has to be clear because this is where I start from. I believe we're alive on the earth on purpose. That we were somebody before we were born, and that being here is like going through a testing ground. To find out who we really are. Maybe not even to prove it to God. I mean, he knows everything. So maybe it's just to prove it to ourselves.

What I'm saying is, I believe in living by the rules and doing things right. I believe in abstinence and honesty and giving a full day's work for a full day's pay. And I believe in doing my best, whatever I do.

I know now what she was thinking I wanted.

I'm lying here looking at the moonlight on my wall, and I know.

I knew it then, too.

I'm not sleeping. You know how the sheets get wound around you? Like you're all tied up. That's me tonight.

I was mad. Offended. All the way home.

But her face stays in my mind. I dream in snatches. Fever dreams. I'm still mad. But not at her.

Because she was right.

At first, I thought, what does she know? Not all guys are that shallow. Maybe some are. But that isn't right. The truth is, there are a lot of jerks out there who wear jockstraps to keep their brains from getting bashed in.

But not me. My mother taught me respect—I'm not going to mess with sex until after I marry somebody. Till

I am committed that much. Marry the person, not just the body. Share a life. Respect the person. Women are people.

But women are people who come dangerously packaged. Their outsides can make you crazy. So you always have to focus on the eyes.

Sometimes it's not that easy.

I always liked to look at Tia, ever since junior high. I don't dare dwell on it. I just look for a second—passing her in the hall—but in that second, it can feel like I took hold of a live wire.

That's how I feel now, hot all over. My palms tingle.

So, what is that? I look, but I have never talked to her. Maybe I smiled at her once. Maybe I don't remember it because of how I feel after I see her.

So she could be right. What if that's why I chose her? What if I don't really care if she's happy?

This scares me.

Alicia

Morgan Weiss. He is the dark angel. Every morning, he stands with his friends at the corner where B hall and C hall meet. And every morning I pass that place. The girls who are with me don't notice, but I look at him whenever I pass. Who could help it?

He stands there, leaning against the wall, sometimes laughing. His eyes are made of shadows; his smile scatters light. His hair falls over his eyes and is beautiful.

Every morning I look at him, and I wonder what it would be like to smoothe that hair away and free those eyes.

Sam

Nikki drives me nuts: "What's wrong? What's wrong with you?"

She wants to know why I'm leaving lunch. She would never understand. I don't understand. So I have to lie to her. I say I'm going to the library. But I go to the parking lot. I'm just sitting in my Jeep. Thinking. I can't stop. Like I'm out of control. Like somebody took the cap off and everything is shooting out.

I have learned something true about myself.

But one truth isn't all truth.

I consider starting up the Jeep right now, just taking

off. But that would mean missing calculus.

I think I envy guys who drink.

Nikki

Peter caught me this afternoon, just before I got on the bus. He was wearing his tennis team whites. "I need to ask you—," he said, panting. He took hold of my arm and pulled me out of line.

"Aren't you supposed to be at practice?" I said, and I laughed—his face was so flushed and his golden curls were a sweaty mess.

"I'm going," he told me impatiently. "I just had to ask you—how's Alicia?"

I hate being put in the middle like this.

"I know," he said, grimacing. "I'm not supposed to be asking. Don't give me any specifics. I just want to know if she's okay."

"She's okay," I said, and started back to the bus.

"She's not okay," he said, blocking my way. "I need you to tell me what happened with her mother. I have to understand why."

"I don't know, Peter," I said. Because I didn't. What

could make a mother leave her family and go off to have some big career? No matter how great a graphic artist she might have been, what kind of choice is that? It wasn't something I wanted to dwell on.

"Look," I told him, keeping my eye on the door of the bus. "Don't worry. Alicia's fine. She hardly ever talks about it."

Peter's face sharpened. "And that doesn't worry you?" His mother's a psychologist; he likes to analyze things. But I am Alicia's friend, and since Alicia doesn't speak to Peter, I was not about to pursue this any further. Especially because the bus door was beginning to close. I pushed past him and banged on it.

"Don't tell her I asked," he said as I got on. Which easily could have meant that he actually wanted me to tell her. Which I was not going to do, as it would only make her mad and could even move her to use harsh language.

I've known Peter since kindergarten, mostly because of Alicia. Peter's always lived across the street from her. When they were little, they were pretty much inseparable.

Peter and Alicia got to be friends in the first place because they were naturally drawn to each other. On the other hand, Alicia and Sam and I were thrown together because we're the only LDS kids—Mormon kids—our age in the school system—we believe the same things and we've always gone to church together.

Without that, I doubt we would have gotten as close as we are—the three of us are so different. Sam is the football scholarship type—letter sweater and pins and all that. Alicia's the service club/student government type. And I'm the scholar and mess-off type. Three separate social classes. Sam is beautiful but focused; Alicia's got this fairy-like delicacy, both in mind and body; and I just run around, collecting people and talking a lot. We see the world in very different ways.

One thing we used to have in common was the kind of families we came from. I've always loved Sam's parents and his family; they are so cool. And I love mine. And I still respect Alicia's father.

It's just, I liked her mom so much, and I never saw it coming.

Sam

So here I am again. Standing by her locker. I can't figure why she gets to her locker so long after everybody else goes home.

I hear her before I see her, the sound of her walking. Those army boots. It echoes between the floor and the ceiling, slamming back and forth between the walls.

When she turns the corner, I get a jab of acid in my stomach. The outside door is at her back; she's a walking shadow against too much light, and I can't see her clearly.

But I know when she sees me; she stops. She stands there, the sun at her back, having no face. I don't need to see to know she is scowling. Her whole body is disgusted. Because I am here.

I see when she shakes her head. She starts walking again, heading for her locker. When she gets big enough in my eyes, she blocks all the light. That's when I finally see her face.

"Go away," she says, biting off the words. She stands as far from me as she can get. It's awkward for her to work the lock at that angle.

I step back. She glances up and, after another minute of fumbling, makes this annoyed sound and moves into the space I have left her.

"Look," I say, wiping one of my palms dry against my jeans, "can we just talk?"

She makes this little disdainful laugh. "Why?" she

asks. She starts jamming books into her locker. "What do you want to say?"

It's my turn. But this is not a conversation. It's some kind of competition, and I don't know the rules.

"What does the nice little Mormon boy want?" she sneers, looking at me now—like she sees right through everything. "Nice little football hero." As though she's spitting on me. She jerks things out of the locker, another book, a black jacket. "Look," she says, slamming the door and snapping the lock together. "I don't have time for this, okay? Go sniff around somebody else."

"You talk like I'm a dog," I say. I'm not leaning against the lockers now. I'm just standing there in space, looking at her. "I'm not."

She takes a breath. "Really," she says. "That's interesting. Good-bye." She starts walking back down the hall.

"Tia," I say. "Could you please—you don't have to make this so hard."

She stops and turns back, and I think again how piercing her eyes can be. "Why do you have to be here all the time?" she asks me, like that's fair. And then she really starts winding up. "What right do you have to say my name? Do you know me? Have you ever said three words to me in your life before this? Look—don't say my name anymore, okay?" And then she spits out this extremely rude phrase.

"I'm talking to you now," I point out.

She stares at me. "Like I'm interested." And starts to turn away.

"Like maybe you should be," I say.

"Why? You going to make me a once-in-a-lifetime offer?" she asks, turning back around slowly. "What could *possibly* come out of your mouth that I care about hearing? You don't know anything about me, and you don't want to. So take off. Go away. Shoo. You understand any of that?"

I am not recording her exact words. She hits me with words I would never speak—weaponized language. I actually have to filter it for myself as it comes in, or it could blow my head off.

And she's walking away again.

"What do you know about me?" I yell after her. "You think you know everything? How do you know *anything*? That's prejudice, Tia." She's still walking. So I say, "Fine. Forget it. Just forget it." Because I'm mad now. And it's my turn to walk off, which I do. My hands are shaking. Mr. Melcher sticks his head out of a doorway, down at the corner.

It's good I look back. Because I see that she is no longer walking. She's standing in the middle of the hall, watching me. So I stop. And we're standing suspended in that long hall, staring at each other. Mr. Melcher's door closes.

She's not going to move.

I take a breath, and I start to walk back to her.

Every step I take is work.

She holds up her hand when she thinks I am close enough. Her face is hard. She is not looking me in the eye. Finally, like she's talking through ice, she says, "Fine. Talk."

And so now it counts. Like there are spotlights and cameras on me. And of course I'm speechless. I'm short of breath. I can't remember how I had any of it worked out. I can't look straight at her. "I wanted to tell you—" She shifts her weight, still staring at something down the hall past me. If we had laser beams coming out of our eyes, the hall would be full of little red lines, fire angles ricocheting off the walls and the floor. But none of them would actually touch either one of us.

Then I say, "I didn't come here for what you think. Not that you're not very . . ." And what am I going to say then? *You're so hot.* I don't think so. "But that's not the reason why." *Because my friends and I thought you needed to be rescued.* "I don't know how to say why," I tell her. I sneak a look at her face.

"Moths to the flame," she says. I can finally feel the laser on my face. I look straight at her. She's not trying to burn holes through me now. For this moment, she's only looking.

I don't have a clue what any of this means.

She nods slowly. "So. Out of the blue," she says, just as slowly, "one day, you simply decide to take a vacation from your good little friends"—she twists the word—"and your nice little life, just to come visit me."

She is waiting. I have the feeling that this is game point. I don't flinch. "I've been looking at you all my life," I admit. "I really like looking at you. But you're right—I don't know anything about you. I realized that, and it didn't seem right. It didn't seem fair."

She shifts her weight again. She is no longer meeting my eyes. She nods. Maybe she's thinking. When she looks at me again, her eyes are hot. "I hate guys like you," she says, her voice in her throat. She turns and walks away.

She gets about three steps and then, unexpectedly,

she laughs. She turns back and gives me this crooked, almost sarcastic smile. "Fine," she says. Then, as if she's making a dare: "You want to get to know me? Then you can give me a ride. Because I'm late." And now she walks straight toward me and then right past me, down the hall toward the parking lot.

"Are you coming?" she says over her shoulder, because I haven't moved yet.

I laugh, wondering what just happened.

And then I follow her.

#4

Sam

I know this place. At least, I have heard of it.

"So, were you going to walk all the way out here?" I ask. We are in Spring City, fifteen miles down the freeway from home, sitting in front of an ancient stone mansion.

"I take the bus," she says.

It has been a long, silent trip. She kept her face turned away from me the whole way, facing into the wind. The windows of my red Jeep are always open. On a good day, I like the top off, the air whipping around me. My stepfather warns me about this: only those green seat belts between you and oblivion. But this is April, and it is too cold for that. So the windows are open.

Her hair did not blow romantically in the wind; it's way too short and stiff for that. She didn't even try to talk. And now we are here. I just don't know why yet.

"Step two," she says. "Are you coming in?"

She says it like a challenge.

"Sure," I say to her, but only because she thinks I won't.

This place doesn't look like a hospital. It looks like history. A building left behind.

We go up the stone steps and across the big porch. Old paint is thick over the door hinges, ragged at the edges of the windows. When we walk inside, our footsteps echo. There are half-empty glass cases in the foyer. And bulletin boards along the walls. The air in here smells like disinfectant.

There is an office window on one side where Tia stops. The woman at the window smiles and hands her a clipboard. Now Tia is talking, chatting with the woman like they are old friends. I look at the bulletin boards while they talk. There is artwork pinned to the cork, crazy artwork in neat lines.

I don't want to be here.

"Come on," Tia says finally. She goes off through another set of double glass doors into a hallway. I follow

her. It's noisy in there—laughter and loud cries and inar-
ticulate sounds. The hair is starting to stand up on the
back of my neck.

"Scared now?" Tia laughs, shooting that *I knew it*
look back over her shoulder. So I have to hurry and catch
up with her, keeping my hands shoved into the deep
pockets of my letter jacket.

We go up a wide, ancient staircase, and down comes
a line of people, really weird people, some of them way
older than we are.

"Tia, how's it going?" a woman says, smiling. I think
this woman must be herding the rest of them, because
she looks fairly normal. "Yeah," says a guy who's got his
fist stuck into one eye. "How's Tia goin'?" You almost
can't understand him.

"Great," Tia says, waving at the guy.

We have come to a landing where the stairs change
direction, and the normal woman stops here. "Who's
this?" she says to Tia, looking me up and down. The
weird people have passed us, on their way down the
stairs.

"Sam." Tia shrugs, like I'm just some insignificant
detail. Then she glances at me and waves toward the
woman. "This is Alma." The weird people have finally

figured out that Alma isn't following them—they're coming back up the stairs.

"Nice to meet you," I remember to say, making myself look at Alma. I say to Tia, "You're late, remember." I don't mean to be rude. I just want to go before the people get back up here.

Tia laughs as though she knows this about me. If she were my sister, I would be rude. Now Tia and Alma are exchanging a look. I hate it when people do that, like they're laughing over your head. And the weird people are starting to crowd around us. It's like being inside a kaleidoscope—all the pieces of these people are there, but they're in the wrong order, and they're the wrong sizes— heads just a little too big, eyes a little too small. It's not like I haven't seen mentally damaged people before. I've just never been this close to them. And they are getting very close, like some of them are practically smashed up against me. They smell like a hospital.

And they're touching me. "Who's this?" a girl asks. The tip of her tongue is stuck in the corner of her mouth. Her face is broad and her dark hair is chopped off short. "C," she says, and puts her hand on the letter on the front of my jacket. She laughs, scratching at the loops on the letter, and says something I can't understand to the guy with the fist stuck in his face. Tia is looking at me, like she's daring me not to step back. So I don't. I look down at the girl and get my breath. "Yeah," I say. "It's soft."

"You're cute," the girl says. The words are very juicy. I smile at her the best I can.

"Thanks," I say.

They're all saying it now—that I'm cute. And somebody says to Tia, "This is your boyfriend." Now, Tia is laughing.

"We've gotta go," Alma says to them. "Say 'bye to Sam."

"Bye, Sam," they say, and they shuffle off obediently. Some wave back at me.

"Bye, Sam," Alma says to me. "It was good of you to come."

This is, of course, not true at all. I know that. The look Tia is giving me says she knows it, too.

"I can't help it," I say to her as I follow her up the next set of stairs. "I've never been to this kind of place before."

"It didn't just suddenly appear on the planet," she says. "You could have come anytime."

"I didn't have a reason to," I tell her, catching up.

"Ah," she says, like she's seeing through me again. We get to the top of the stairs.

"You can't cut me a break, can you?" I say. Now I'm a little torqued. I get enough of this stuff from my step-father.

"You're here, aren't you?" Tia says, and keeps walking.

She finally stops in front of a door and knocks on it. Evidently she hears what she expects to hear, and opens the door. "Come on," she says. So I follow her into the room.

The first thing I see is the round window at the end of the room. The sunlight is streaming through it past a pattern of leaves.

Nikki

We had our first project meeting today. I had to take the bus home to get my car, because, of course, the meeting had to be at Camarga's instead of at my house: "How much memory does your computer have?" he asked, and when I couldn't tell him, that was the end of the discussion.

Brian lives out by Alicia's, in the Tree Avenues. It's not an especially rich area. Not that I expected the Camargas would be rich. Or maybe I did. What kind of houses do nerds usually live in? Like I would know. Camarga's was a middle-sized, normal house—not showy, but nice. The lawn was neat; the whole neighborhood was neat, very landscaped, with stone walks curving up to the doors.

When I knocked, a tall woman with short, extremely red hair came to the door.

"I'm here for Brian," I told her. At which she looked surprised.

"Really," she said. "You're not here to see James? You look so young."

"Brian Camarga," I told her, starting to worry I was at the wrong house, and feeling a little insulted. "I'm a senior," I added, just so she would know.

"Well," she said, and she laughed. "You kids get younger all the time. Why don't you wait in here while I find Brian?" And there I was, alone in the Camargas' front hall, with nothing to look at but Brian Camarga's living room. Which, by the way, didn't look a thing like the living room at my house.

"This is not a home," my mother is known to say, looking over our place. "It's a workshop with furniture." We have interestingly diverse furniture, and there are little quilts hanging on all the walls. We've got books, paper, art supplies, and fabric piled up everywhere. We like it like that—all our tools and raw materials very close at hand. Well, maybe my mom doesn't especially like it.

Brian's house has hardwood floors with neat rugs here and there and floral, formal furniture that matches the drapes. And the smell at the Camargas' is different.

I can't tell you exactly what my house smells like— wood and Christmas and onions and mint? Brian's house smells like a craft store, like those candles you get in glass jars. One weird thing I noticed when we were overseas was the smell. Paris didn't smell like home—diesel fuel and hot crepes and the river. I was amazed at how displaced I felt because of that. Smell turns out to be a big part of how you feel about a place. I was definitely feeling like I'd stepped into another country, standing in the Camargas' hall, breathing in their smell.

"Brian says you're going to have to work in his room," his mother announced. "Sorry. It's not the best thing, but that's where the computer is." She started shepherding me along the hall. "It's in the basement," she said, pointing down some wide stairs. "And I'm afraid it's a mess." The stairway walls were painted a nice medium gold, and they were covered with framed family photos. We came out into the family room.

"We sort of live down here," she apologized. I didn't

see any mess. The place looked like a furniture store. There was a red-haired boy lounging on the couch, fiddling with a video game. "This is James," Brian's mother said politely. James didn't look up. He was actually not at all bad looking for somebody his age, which took me a little by surprise—and which, by the way, half proved my Great Idea.

Mrs. Camarga had gone down a short hallway and was waiting for me. "I guess it'll be okay if you keep the door open," she said, sounding a little nervous—like she had to worry about Brian and me being alone together.

She stepped back, and I got my first look at Brian Camarga's bedroom. Right away, I thought, Where does this guy sleep? The place looked like some kind of FBI operations center.

"You're late," Brian said, without looking up. His mother grimaced apologetically and went away. Brian was sitting in an upholstered office chair, hunched over a keyboard, his whole attention fixed on the screen of a huge monitor. I stepped over a box of parts, caught my foot on a random cable, and barely saved myself from crashing into a rack of blinking components by grabbing the back of Brian's chair.

The chair swung around and Brian said a very rude

thing—not a normal rude thing, but some nerd thing I didn't understand—and jerked his chair back. "You pulled the keyboard out," he whined, shoving the plug back in like it was some kind of emergency. And then he sat there muttering to himself, jabbing at the keys, completely focused on the screen.

There was no place for me to sit, so I just waited—until I realized what he was doing.

"You're playing a *game?*" I asked him. "I was freaking out because I was *late*."

"Shhhh," he hissed, and leaned closer to the screen. I had to admire his typing skills.

A few minutes later, he said, "Ha!" and his hands came off the keyboard with a flourish. Something blew up on the screen; then it went dark until a line of fiery golden runes came up. "Yesss," he said. He reached over and pushed a button. Rubbing his hands together, he spun around in the chair and announced, "I'm off."

"You were on the Net," I sneered. He looked at me like, *Duh.*

"You have no idea what I just accomplished," he said to me, his voice dripping with pity.

"You just wasted five minutes of my life playing some computer game," I said.

"Some computer game?" he said, gaping at me. "*Some* computer game? This"—he swung the chair around again, holding his two hands out to the screen—"is my work."

"Your work," I echoed, unimpressed.

"I've got two years invested in this game," he said. "I play six characters. *Six*. One of them is a scion mage with twelve honors on the sixteenth level."

I think at that point I was supposed to press my hand to my heart.

"*The Erissian Wilderness* has a worldwide player-ship," Brian said very patiently, like he was explaining it to his grandmother. "You know how much somebody in Sweden just offered me for Greunnel? For just one of my characters? The least of all of them?"

"Offered you?" I said.

"Five thousand dollars, my friend," Brian said, pointing at me. "Five thousand American dollars. Which is what's going to buy my books at MIT."

"Somebody offered you money for some character you made up?" I asked, narrowing my eyes at him.

"Somebody," he said, "who does not want to have to cross the Wastes of the Imperium himself, which can save him as much as two years."

"Five thousand dollars?" I murmured. "For a game?"

"For *The Erissian Wilderness,*" he corrected me.

"Whoa," I said politely.

Brian nodded. I don't know if I have mentioned it before, but Brian makes this annoying noise, kind of a grinding snort, like he's clearing something really disgusting out of his throat. I think it's a Tourette syndrome thing. He made it now and shoved his glasses up against his face.

"You ought to sit down," he said. I looked around for something to sit on.

He made an impatient noise and left the room. A second later he came back with a wooden stool, which he put down beside his big chair. "You can sit there," he said, and put his own narrow little self back in the nice padded chair.

"Well?" he said, blinking up at me and evidently missing my glare. "Sit down."

So I sat.

"The project," he began, "is as follows: we are going to create an interactive website that will explain the functions of messenger RNA through text and 3-D animation. I have already started modeling the ribosome, and I have Calvin's preliminary sketch of the site design. What we need to do is finish the basic design and then script it and start writing the HTML."

I just looked at him.

"So which parts do you want to do?" he asked me.

Now I blinked.

"You want to start with the scripting?" he prompted.

"Like," I said, "dialogue and stuff?"

"Dialogue?" he said blankly.

"You know," I offered, "narration?"

"I meant the script for the animation," he said, staring at me. "Like, the person calls up the site, and then what happens?"

"Oh," I said, feeling my face go hot. "Well, you start on the home page, and then you can—are we going to have more than one page of this? I mean, of course, we have to, don't we?"

"I'd think so," he said, looking grim.

"Well, if it's going to be an animation," I said, "then we ought to start with a strand of DNA in the first place, shouldn't we? I mean, we have to. And we could make the sections different colors according to segment. Can you do it 3-D? Because I think that would look really cool."

"Not a problem," he said.

"So then, you have to show the DNA doing the

replication—isn't this going to be hard?" I had suddenly gotten a feel for the size of the thing that Brian and Calvin had been planning. "This project is going to be pretty complex," I said slowly. "And it's not like we have a whole lot of time before it's due."

Brian smiled and patted his keyboard. "Complexity," he said happily, "is my middle name."

#5

Sam

"This is Jonathan," Tia says. She is sitting on a bed with him. The round window is behind them. The light around them makes it so I can't see him clearly at first.

"He has Down's syndrome," she goes on, "but he's pretty functional—aren't you, Jon?"

Jonathan is now nodding. I have moved so that I can see him better. He is grinning at me so hard, his eyes have disappeared.

"This is Tia," Jonathan tells me. When he speaks, it's like he's got something in his mouth, like his tongue is bigger than it should be. "She's my sister." Jon puts his arm around Tia, beaming at her, then beaming at me.

"You're pretty lucky," I tell him.

"Yes," he agrees. "I am."

"Well, let's take a look at what you've been doing," Tia says, and with their arms still around each other, they get up and go to what I now see is a desk. It is a tiny room. Like a dorm: two beds, two desks, two chairs, two closets. It's very neat. Jon's bed has a thermal blanket on it. The other bed is covered with a quilt.

"This is our private time," Jon tells me while Tia looks at the things on the desk. Then he says, "You can come look." So I do. It's his homework, I think—writing and drawing and some other stuff.

It's impossible to tell how old Jonathan is. His body is short, but it's stocky and sturdy looking. His face—I don't know how to describe it. Strange. Wrong. The eyes are too small, too far apart, and they are red and runny. His head is too big, and his forehead is too high. His skin seems weirdly elastic. But when he smiles, everything works together. Since he is smiling most of the time, I begin to relax.

"You can sit down," he says graciously. So I do. Then he sits right next to me and takes my hand, giving me that weird angel smile. Tia watches all of this with one corner of her lip tucked up. I pat Jon's hand and glare at her.

"Which book?" she asks, not talking to me.

"*Jesse*," Jon says. "In the shelf." So she goes to the shelf and gets out a kid's picture book.

"'*When Jesse Came Over the Sea*,'" Tia reads. Jonathan immediately slides off the bed onto the floor, sitting with his legs stretched out in front of him.

"You sit down," he instructs Tia, twisting himself to pat the bed next to me.

"But you won't be able to see," she points out.

"You can show me," he reassures her, then puts his head back, closes his eyes, and folds his hands peacefully across his chest.

So she sits down, and she reads him this book.

Every so often, there are loud sounds in the hallway. The spiky, distant voices never go away. Leaf shadows dance on the wall across the room. Tia reads and shows us the pictures, and goes on reading. She reads well, taking her time.

Jonathan is obviously very happy.

It isn't until she says "I've got to go" that it all hits the fan.

"He never wants me to leave," Tia tells me later, walking out to the Jeep. "And it's like he can't hide his feelings. If he's happy, he's happy. If he's not, he's not. There's nothing fake about him.

"Don't you think most people are fake?" she asks me. "Civilization is a fake. Don't you ever wish you could just go ahead and throw a fit when you feel like it?" She turns away, laughing. "Look who I'm asking."

"What's that supposed to mean?" I ask. She gets me mad so fast.

She smirks at me that way she does, like she's daring me to come in closer. I don't know if that's supposed to make me want to, or if it's supposed to warn me off.

"Mr. Perfect," she says smugly. She climbs into the Jeep—which she is able to do because I open the flipping door for her.

I walk around to my side, clenching my teeth.

She gives me that look again as I get in. I just shake my head and pull down my seat belt.

"Like now," she says. "How are you feeling right now?"

I make an exasperated noise and look at her. "What do you want?" I say.

She nods. "So repressed," she says sarcastically. "I'll bet you throw plenty of fits when you don't get what you want." She laughs. Her laugh is full of broken glass.

"Just tell me where you live," I say. And she does. And I take her home.

It is another silent trip. We end up in front of a large house in an older, but still nice, neighborhood. There is a porch, and wide windows across the front. The Jeep has stopped moving, but she doesn't get out right away. I look at her.

"You did okay," she says.

"Big surprise," I say.

"Well, it was obviously hard for you," she says. "I don't think you're used to broken people."

I don't have anything to say to that.

"You were scared," she said. "Admit it."

"Fine," I say. "I was nervous at first."

"You were scared," she says, not quite mocking.

"Everybody's scared of something," I tell her.

She laughs. "Not me," she says. "There's nothing left."

Alicia

I do a lot of the cooking around here these days. And I have to make sure that Ann gets picked up. It's not what I should be doing. I should be like Nikki, who can come and go whenever she wants to.

I don't have that kind of freedom. I didn't used to have anybody depending on me, but now they both do, Dad and Ann. Sometimes I feel like I'm the only one who's doing any thinking around here.

"I probably shouldn't be saying these things to you," he said to me the other night. And I said to him, "Dad, if you can't talk to me, then who can you talk to?"

I meant it then. But now I don't know.

"I'm old and I'm sick," he said. "Who's going to be interested in a future with that? I don't know how anybody expects me to be able to start over again."

My father has always been so dependable—like the earth, or our house. He holds everything up, makes everything normal. He has his own business, and he works really hard. He's always got everything organized. He's always known what to do. Even the past month, he's more or less held us together. Even so, it's all coming apart. And now, I'm afraid he's coming apart, too.

I don't understand why he thinks that nobody would be interested in him. But more to the point, why would he say that? Why is he even worrying about somebody being interested in him?

I just wish he hadn't said it.

Sam

I can't settle down to study.

Dad came home. Before he even said hello, he yelled at me for not taking out the trash. It made me furious.

But why? Why should I be mad?

I'm supposed to take out the trash every night. Mom already asked me three times. So why did I have to pitch a fit when he yelled?

I'm still mad.

Alicia called tonight. "You were so quiet this afternoon," she said. "Something wrong?"

What should be wrong? Tia's house was in a nice part of town. Why did that surprise me? Why does it still?

Alicia

If they honestly thought that Ann and I couldn't hear, they must have been incredibly naive. They always fought at night, down in their room. I guess they thought it'd be private down there, as though there are no vents, as if they thought the walls and floor are ten feet thick. I heard all the things she said to him. Everything was his fault. She must have said the word *controlling* a million times. "You have never listened to how I feel," she said. "You always thought you had the right to decide whether or not to 'let' me take care of my own money."

I almost wanted to laugh at that one. I remember the fight they had after she'd taken over the checkbook for two months. She bounced fourteen checks. How could anybody bounce that many checks?

The fighting used to make Ann cry, and then I had to go sit with her until she could fall asleep. But it wasn't always that way. I'm almost eighteen years old. I remember. We used to be happy.

"I got married too young," my mother said to me just before she finally left. "I never got a chance to know what I wanted. Never, never let a man tell you what you want. Because he will. He'll just take over everything if you let him. It's the way men are, having to control everything."

I suppose she meant Daddy. It makes me feel like we must have lived with two different people. I never saw any of these things in him. I never heard him be rude. It always seemed to me that he listened to her. We do have rules in our house, and my father enforces them. But so does my mother. My mother raises her voice at us all the time.

Oh.

She used to raise her voice. When she lived here. A month ago.

I never heard my father speak harshly to her unless they were both angry and shouting. So how is it that he's the only bad person in all of this?

Now she lives in L.A. But he's here. With Ann and me.

I can't help thinking that's significant.

Nikki

I talked to Alicia on the phone tonight. I tried, but I couldn't pry the truth out of her. What's the big deal, anyway? I told her who I chose. She's defensive about this, which makes me very suspicious. This is so not her, keeping secrets. Alicia and I used to tell each other everything.

When I finally gave up and guessed Peter, she got very stiff with me. I don't get this, either. All these years, and she's never breathed a word about why she suddenly started hating him. The only thing she'll say is that she can't stand betrayal.

This thing with her mom, it's changed her. I was thinking

about that tonight, and I started watching my own mom. She was just doing the stuff she usually does: yelling at somebody to set the table, complaining about having to be the one who cooks. She moves through the house so naturally. It's almost like a dance: reach, bend, turn, open, close, yell, praise, go in, go out. She never stops.

And all the time, we're following her around, chattering away about somebody at school did this or said that, or maybe telling her about a great skateboard triumph. Can she really care about all of this? Not that she's always actually listening. But somehow, she knows most of my friends, even the ones she's never met. She remembers things about them, as if my life matters to her.

She keeps the books for my father's business, makes artsy quilts, does church stuff, does everything, all the time whining and complaining and feeling guilty because she's such a failure. I don't tell her—it would be like saying thank you to the sun for shining, or to the air for being there to breathe—how much all of this means to me.

My parents fight. It scares me when they do. You never know what parents may end up doing. Nobody guessed about Alicia's mom. Not even my mother saw it coming. Or if she did, she never said anything to me about it.

I don't think I could stand betrayal either.

Maybe Peter is right. Maybe it would be better if Alicia would talk, or scream, or cry, or break things. She's got to feel like tearing the whole world apart with her hands. But she's so quiet. I'm afraid she'll someday just spontaneously combust, and that will be it. And who will be there for her when that happens?

#6

Alicia

I want to sing the song of Morgan Weiss.

I do not know him. The first time I saw him was in ninth grade, and even as early as that, our worlds were so far apart, there was no intersecting point at which we could meet. His friends, my friends. Basic math, college algebra. He smoked, even back then.

Still.

Nikki has no idea. Morgan is a glint imprisoned in shadow. I harbor my hopes for him the way you'd cup your hand around a flame. I don't need anyone else's opinions about this. It is my own private leap of faith.

I won't tell you about how he dresses. I won't tell you about who his friends are or about the rumors, because all of that would give you the wrong idea. You have to look into his face to see what he is. Every time I have ever looked into his face, I ached inside my chest.

It hasn't happened often. But one day, one morning last fall, just about the time when the leaves had turned and the air had gone crisp, I was walking to class with Charlotte and Renée, and we passed his corner. I was carrying a big book, too big for my backpack, and so I had it in my arms, folded against me. I looked up, and there he was. I could hardly see him through the press of his friends. Then the crowd shifted, and suddenly, there was his face. He was laughing, and then he looked right into my eyes.

I swear, a bolt of energy passed between us. His eyes met mine, and I could barely stand the intensity of the connection.

"What is it?" my friends asked as we passed him by. I know I had staggered a little. "Alicia, are you all right?"

But one word spoken aloud would have ruined the moment.

If I say that now our souls are linked, it will sound as though I am overly romantic. But I will tell you that something happened in that moment. Some understanding passed between us.

Morgan is a lost boy. But not so lost that there is no light in his eyes. They are eyes that cry for beauty and truth. Obviously, the place in which he lives, his world, is starving him. I don't know anything about his family, but it seems to me that he must be very alone. That morning, I swore: if there is ever any opportunity for me to do it, I will be there for him. I will be his bridge. I will hold on and I will never let go.

Nikki

I'm worried about what's going to happen when Brian finally realizes that I have no idea how to write HTML. I got a book about it today out of the computer lab. *HTML for Dummies*. I figured that sounded about right. I'm reading it, but I can't say it's making a lot of sense to me. I use computers all the time for research and writing and e-mail. I'm just not a programmer.

Brian seems to like my ideas about the animation sequence. I've done a couple of rough sketches. It's kind of unfair; I know the science, but I look stupid because I don't know how to do what we're doing.

I read the darned book all the way through lunch

today. Sam and Alicia didn't seem to mind. They were talking about somebody in their English class—yawn. The project is due the Monday after prom weekend. That's only a couple of weeks.

I don't know how I'm going to pull this off.

I hear that Calvin Sweeney is really mad at me.

Sam

I went to bed last night, hoping it was over. I can pass her in the hall now and wave. Maybe say "Hi." Isn't that enough? Can't I be done now?

But no.

It's indefensible: for the third day, I am waiting by her locker. I'm a sitting duck. I know how she's going to look at me. I know how I'm going to feel. I hate being confused. It's like inching along a ledge on a cliff face: you don't believe you could actually fall, but you still don't dare look down.

She comes around the corner. But this time, she hardly hesitates when she sees me. Instead, she gets this superior little smile and does that walk of hers, like she doesn't wear Nazi boots for nothing.

"So," she says when she gets close enough. "I thought I'd never see you again."

"Why?" I ask her, like an idiot.

"I thought I scared you off yesterday," she says. She spins in her combination and jerks the locker open.

"Yeah," I say. "Well. I guess not."

"I guess not," she says. She starts messing with books. Then she pulls out her coat. "So, what do you want?" she asks me. She's not smiling.

I shrug. "Thought you'd like a ride," I say. "It's cold out there today. Windy."

"Well," she says, and turns away, putting on her coat. "I guess," she says.

So I take her there again. At least now I know what to expect. I mean, I'm still uncomfortable; somebody's bound to end up drooling on me or something. And there are a few people in that place who really need to learn how to wipe their noses, which grosses me out. But I think I'm basically okay with it now. The Scriptures say you have to take care of people like this, that it's more than just a good thing. I am too ashamed of how I feel about it to stop going at this point.

Today, the same kind of things go on, weird people doing weird stuff. Maybe it didn't creep me out so entirely this time. I'm still uncomfortable. I don't know what to do. What to say to them. So I watch the people who work there, trying to get a feel for it.

But she doesn't cut me a break.

"You did real good today," she says on the way home. She says it with this smart-aleck little pat on my knee.

"I'm trying," I tell her.

"Yeah," she says. "So, why?"

"Why what?" I ask, even though I know what she's asking.

"Why should you try?" she asks.

I shrug again. "Because it's a good thing to do," I say, which is almost completely true.

"So," she says, "if I weren't a factor here, you'd still be doing this?"

"I don't know," I say. "There are lots of good things to do. I suppose you have to have a reason to choose which one."

She laughs. "You're a real Boy Scout," she says. And then, like it suddenly dawns on her, "You probably are. You really are a Boy Scout, aren't you?"

And suddenly I'm ashamed. Why? What possible shame could be in this? I hate it that she makes me feel this way. "I'm an Eagle Scout," I tell her. I can feel my face go red.

"Really, " she says, and starts laughing, like that's the funniest thing she's ever heard.

I always end up mad when I'm with her.

"It's just so perfect," she says, wiping her eyes.

Not angry like I want to hit somebody. I can't explain it. She humiliates me.

"Why do you do this?" I ask her.

"What?" she says.

"Why do you make fun of everything about me?"

She laughs again, one short, hollow-sounding laugh.

"Because you're a cartoon character," she says. "You're fake. "

"I'm fake," I say.

"When you let me off at my house, and you drive down and turn the corner, you just—disappear. And then they bring you out tomorrow at school, with your little letter jacket and your clean shirt. I'm surprised you don't wear loafers or saddle shoes or something."

I do not answer this.

"Someday," she says, not laughing now, "this little act you put on is going to get holes in it. And then we'll see what's really down there, won't we? Listen, Boy Scout," she says, leaning toward me as I pull up at her house.

"Listen, nice little Mormon boy—nobody's this nice. Nobody. And I'm not going to let you pull this on me. Okay?" She straightens up and opens the door and jumps out of the Jeep. Then she turns and gives me this saucy up-yours kind of look and walks away.

I'm grateful for my anger, because that walk of hers could drive me wild.

Nikki

I went to Brian's again. We have to meet every day from now on. He's already started modeling the DNA strand, which he says won't take that long. And his ribosome is so cool—so completely 3-D, you think you could poke a dent in it with your finger.

When I told him it reminded me of a little docking unit at a space station, he made this rude face. "That's the whole point," he said.

"I thought the point was to make it look like a ribosome," I said.

"Ribosomes," he said in a completely insulting tone, "look like space stations."

"I see," I said. "I guess you ought to know."

"Do you even watch *Star Trek*?" he asked me.

"Yes, I watch *Star Trek*," I said. "Although I don't see what that has to do with it. Anyway, if you're talking science fiction, *Star Trek* was never as good as *Star Wars.*"

"*That*," he said, "is certainly debatable. And your very statement tells me that you do not, in fact, actually watch *Star Trek*. You just sit through it."

"I have never been tempted to go to a convention, if that's what you mean," I said haughtily.

"And I suppose you've never even heard of *Babylon Five*," he said.

"Certainly I have," I told him. "My mother watches it religiously."

"It's not on anymore," he informed me smugly.

"It's in syndication," I informed him—I can out-smug Camarga any day of the week.

"Hardly the same thing." He sniffed, waving his hand. "But that's beside the point. You will note," he went on, "how every ribosome is designed to fit the corresponding RNA exactly. Which indicates the high level of specialized functional design that characterizes life on this planet."

"I know," I said. "It's beautiful: each little ship goes down into its ribosome, and the little hoses extend right into the exact ports on the RNA—how are we ever going to animate all that?"

"I seriously think," Brian said, thoughtfully tweaking his ribosome, "that all of this had to have been carefully, deliberately designed by somebody."

"Yeah," I said to him, "well, me too. But that doesn't answer my question. Unless you can get the same guy to spontaneously generate this webpage."

He laughed. I'd actually made him laugh. I used to think that Brian Camarga's laugh was not a terrifically pleasant sound. But now, it made me laugh. And there we were, laughing together. "That was a good one," he said. And then he sobered up, scowling at his monitor screen.

"We'll have to simplify the structures," he said sadly.

"Yeah," I said, chewing on my bottom lip. Then I sat up straight. "Or maybe not. We'll just show it in cross section. You show the ribosome, and the kid can click on it, and it opens up—and *voilà*, the kid sees how it works inside."

He did his snort thing and nodded.

"What is that?" I asked him. "Why do you do that?"

"What?" he asked me.

"That sound," I said, and did something like it so he understood.

"I have this post-nasal sinus thing," he said absently,

adjusting the wire frame. So he actually *was* clearing gross stuff out of his throat.

"You know," he said, "you have good ideas. I have to admit, you've really surprised me."

"You thought I was stupid," I said.

"Well, partly that." He messed with the keyboard. "Mostly, I didn't think we'd be able to communicate."

I made a rude noise. "And why would you think that?"

He shrugged and wrinkled up his nose. "You're just so—I thought you were kind of silly, that's all."

"I'm not silly," I said, offended.

"Yes, you are," he said. "You're silly and you're loud and you're always calling attention to yourself. Always flitting around, talking to people. You just don't seem to be a serious person, that's all."

"I am, too, serious," I told him.

"See?" he said. "You're loud."

"When I'm being insulted," I pointed out.

"Well, don't be insulted," he said. "Serious people generally don't expect that much out of babes, that's all. But you were different than I expected."

"Babes?" I said.

"All that aside," he went on, "the truth is, you don't have the tools you need for this project."

It was the simple truth.

"But—," I said, an idea dawning in my silly, babish head, "this project is cool enough, and complex enough, I bet we could talk Mr. Webb into letting us do it as a foursome. You think Calvin would come back on board?"

He brightened right up. "Good idea," he said. Then his face fell. "But he'd have to bring skater-man Kelly Smythe with him."

"You'd have to let me keep doing designs," I warned him. "I don't want to be shut out."

"If we have Calvin working on the HTML," he said, "we'd go fast enough, and I could teach you to do some of this modeling. It's not that hard, once you know what you're doing."

"You have to call Calvin," I told him. "Calvin really hates me."

"Yes," he said, grimacing. He shoved his glasses back up his nose. "That's going to be a problem."

We looked at each other. "Two weeks," he said. "We've only got two weeks."

#7

Sam

Term paper.

I can't write.

I can't stop thinking.

At first, being around Tia—it was fire. All feeling. Not much thinking.

But every time I talk to her, the thinking gets more.

I wish the fire would go away.

It's not just Tia. Everything is weird right now. I have a great family. I love my mom. It's my dad—my stepfather; I can't do anything right.

He used to be our home teacher. But I need to explain that. In our church, every family is given two home teachers: two men who watch over the family. They make sure there's enough food. They help you pick up your car at the shop. They help if somebody's sick or whenever you ask. They become your friends. My stepfather wasn't married then. His first wife died of cancer and he didn't have kids. He'd been alone awhile. He and another guy were assigned to be our home teachers when I was about six.

When I was seven, my first father left for good.

I don't remember being that upset about it. He'd never been home much anyway. It was the home teacher who always took me to the father's and son's stuff. He was the one who helped me make my Pinewood Derby car in Cub Scouts. So I wasn't real cut up when my first father decided he didn't need us.

But my mother was. I still remember. I guess she called the home teachers after she found out. Maybe she was afraid of doing something terrible. So they turned up at the door, and she started kicking things and yelling at them. "Men are such jerks. I did *everything*," she said. "I held up my end of that marriage." I distinctly remember her saying, "You couldn't even get him to take the trash out around here, but he can step out with *her*?" It made a deep impression on me. I think it made a deep impression on my stepfather, too. Which may be why the trash is such a point with him.

Now he wants me to get a job. He thinks I'm spoiled. He thinks I should pay for my own gas and car insurance. I'm mad when he says I'm spoiled. But I can see why he wants me to pay for those things. Here's the problem: when could I work? All fall I had football practice. That's like a job, since it got me a scholarship. It's the same as working for money to go to college. And I have church responsibilities. And these classes.

My mom says grades are more important than earning money right now. Dad says why do I need straight A's when I already have the scholarship? Then they argue. It's not serious arguing, but it makes me tired.

When he first came into my life, my dad made everything different. He was always there, fixing things, playing with me. He made my mother laugh. He always did what he said he was going to do. We were really good friends. Now, he doesn't understand that I have a life, too. I have my own responsibilities.

I'm supposed to be taking AP's in a few weeks. I'll never get my head that clear. Tia takes up too much time. I can't keep going with her every day. But now I've set this precedent, and I don't know how to get out of it.

And anyway—I don't want to get out of it.

Not yet.

Nikki

Tomorrow we meet with Calvin and Kelly for the first time. This is assuming that Mr. Webb hasn't got a problem with the double-team idea. But he's pretty reasonable, so I'm not worried.

I talked to Brian about the prom today, just wondering if he'd asked anybody yet. He laughed. He said he had absolutely no interest in dances, thank you very much. I said, "So, you wouldn't enjoy a fun night dressing up and going to the dance and hanging out with your friends?" He pointed out that it would be hard to hang out with his friends at a dance, since none of his friends go to dances.

Besides, he isn't comfortable with girls. It seems that you can't talk to them. He has promoted me; I am no longer a girl. I am, instead, a person whose mother watches *Babylon Five*.

Alicia

I almost talked to him today. I have to be careful about it, because of his friends. And because of mine. It was when I left lunch. I was walking out toward C hall, thinking about my English class. Then I saw him by his locker. Nobody was with him, and Nikki had gone to gym. The hall hadn't quite started to fill up before sixth.

When I see Morgan, the palms of my hands always start to tingle. I think of talking to him, and my heart begins to panic. I was walking very slowly, trying to get up my courage, when suddenly, someone said my name.

It was Peter, following me. He said my name so loudly, I was humiliated, afraid Morgan had heard and would know that I'd been standing there, looking at him. So I started walking, trying to ignore Morgan as he slammed his locker shut.

Peter said my name again, but I didn't answer. I could feel him following me, and I was angry. Whenever I'm around Peter, I'm angry.

When I got to my class, I stopped. When I opened the door, I looked back, but there was no Peter behind me.

I am still mad about it, sitting here in my window, looking at the moon. It hangs over Peter's house like some kind of omen. I wish Peter's house could just disappear. Whenever I remember to see it, I feel pain.

I wish my mother would hurry and come back. I see

now that I used to be all tied up with being my mother's girl. This year has changed that. I am cut adrift. When she calls on the phone, I can tell she wants me still to be the same, her girl. And part of me wants that, too. But another part of me knows it's impossible. I belonged to the person she was, the person who would never leave me, but that person chose to change. And so I had to change. The bonds between us have been shredded to sorry ribbons.

Still, maybe there's a chance it could work again—if she came back. This time, I would talk to her more. Maybe if I had talked to her more, or listened more, none of this would have happened.

#8

Nikki

This has been one lousy Friday. Mr. Webb gave us the go-ahead, but that was the high point. I tried to tell my "best friends" about it at lunch; they couldn't bother to pretend to listen. They don't even talk to each other anymore. I don't know what's happening to us, but it seems like we're suddenly on different buses, headed in different directions.

Then I went to Brian's. Calvin and Kelly were already there. I could tell within seconds that this was not going to be fun. Kelly is such a skater. He doesn't focus. He just kept messing with things, and Brian was constantly saying, "Don't touch that. Don't touch that." *So* annoying. Then Calvin got a look at the project.

"This isn't what we planned," he complained.

"It's better now," Brian told him.

"No, it isn't," Calvin said. "It was better before. Before *she* messed it up." Whine, whine, whine. It turned into this big fight, during which Calvin kept referring to me as *she*, like I wasn't sitting right there. Finally, Calvin stalked out of the house, and I had to drive Kelly all the way to his place.

When I finally got home, I had a message to call Alicia. So I went upstairs and called her. I told her how mad I was about the fight, and I complained about Calvin and how I can't possibly start a new project from scratch all by myself at this point.

"Yeah," she kept saying. "Yeah."

Well, I can tell when people are just being polite. So I felt stupid, and I stopped. I made myself ask, "What's going on with you?"

"Nothing," she said after a moment. Just in case you don't already know this, any time a female answers any question with the word *nothing,* she is lying. Especially if she says it after a small pause. The word *nothing* actually means "something significant which you had better keep trying to figure out if you care *anything* at all about this relationship."

"How's your dad?" I tried.

"He's not doing that great," she said.

"Oh," I said. "And you?" I asked her. "Are you doing okay?" *As opposed to me, who has to deal with Calvin the Whino?*

No. Silence is a "no."

"Nikki," she said finally. "You know how we always say that, sooner or later, my mom will get over it and come home?" Alicia said.

"Yeah?" I said.

"Well, my dad got served with divorce papers today," she told me. "She has a lawyer and everything. My dad hasn't even thought about getting a lawyer."

"Oh," I said, and sat down.

"At Christmas, we were a family, Nikki," Alicia said. "A forever family. It never, ever occurred to me that it could change." She stopped. When she started again, her voice was broken. "I can't believe this is real. But every morning I wake up, and she's still gone. She's not coming back, Nikki. Not after this."

"Hey," I said hopefully. "Maybe she's just trying to scare him."

"Well, she's scaring me," Alicia said.

And me, I thought.

"If that's the kind of person she is now," Alicia went on, "then she's nothing like I thought she was. So either way, my life is smashed. Murdered. I don't know what I'm going to do. I don't know how I'm going to sleep. I don't know how I'm going to wake up. Maybe I don't even want to wake up."

"Don't say that, Alicia," I said. "I don't ever want to hear you say that."

"This is killing my dad," she said. "I can't talk to him about it. I'm all alone." And then she stopped completely.

"Well," I said, taking a deep breath, "I'm here for you."

And I almost really meant it.

After that conversation, the evening just got worse.

All the little kids had finally gone to bed. My brother Jesse, who graduated last year, was in the back bedroom, and I was in the den, doing homework.

My parents were talking in the kitchen. I heard Jesse get up and go down the hall to the bathroom. My parents had been getting louder by degrees. I couldn't hear any actual words at first because the kitchen door was closed, but after a while, they got so loud the door became academic. Back and forth it was going, back and forth: "Well, if you hadn't—," "Well, if you *had*—." I had no idea what they were mad about; they'd been fine at dinner.

The kitchen door opened, and they came out into the den.

My mother was not exactly yelling, but very close. "Okay, then—what *that* means is that you're not responsible for what matters to me, but I'm supposed to be *completely* responsible for *everything* that matters to you."

"Nooooo, that's *not* what it means," my father, who does not know the meaning of normal speaking voice, shouted back at her.

"Well, what else could it mean, Tim?" She gets very queenly at times like these. "You may not *want* it to mean that, but that's *exactly* what it means. You can't do something and then say it doesn't mean what it plainly means—what anybody, *anybody* would say it meant—"

I couldn't stand it. I couldn't stand another second of it.

"This is the stupidest argument I have *ever* heard," I said, getting up off the floor. "You should just hear yourselves. I *hate* it when you do this. I just *hate* it."

They stopped all right. And then they stood there staring at me.

"Just stop yelling!" I yelled. "You sound like a couple of bratty little kids. You sound worse than *we* do."

"Good night *nurse*, Nikki," my mother shouted. "Why don't you just go put yourself right in the line of fire?"

"And we are *not* yelling," my father informed me, hollering.

"I mean it," I warned. "I'm sick of this."

Jesse materialized in the hall doorway. "You're waking everybody up," he informed us. We could hear Sterling howling in his room.

"It's not *my* fault," I told him.

"All of you," Jesse said calmly.

"Well, *excuse* me," my mother said. "Your father and I were just working something out—"

"Oh, that's a great way of working things out," I said with *awful* sarcasm. "That's a *great* way to communicate. Thank you for the fine *example*. Thank you for waking everybody up. Thank you for *scaring* me to death."

"Scaring you," my mother said. "Why would you be scared?"

"Why do you think?" I bellowed. "Why do you think?" And then I burst into tears.

"I'll take care of Sterling," Jesse said, dematerializing.

"Oh, for heaven's sake," my mother said, and gathered me in. "Alicia," she said quietly, over my head.

"Ah," I heard my father say.

"You sound like you hate each other," I wailed into her shoulder.

"No, we don't," she said. "We sound like we're ticked off."

"Yes, you do," I said.

"Well, sometimes we do hate each other," my mother said.

"No, we don't," my father said. "*I* never do."

I could feel my mother turning to send him a mean look. "But it's only temporary," she went on. "You think just because two people are parents, they can live in the same space and never get aggravated? Come here." She pulled me over to the couch and sat me down. "Here," she said, offering me a paper napkin, which I used immediately. "You kids fight all the time," she went on. "Do you hate each other?"

I didn't say anything, but I was thinking, *sometimes.*

"So your father and I are supposed to be perfect?"

"Yes," I said. "You are. And besides, you punish us when we fight."

"That's because we're clearly in charge of *you*," my father said, glaring at my mother.

"It's not like we get mad that often," she said calmly.

"You don't ever have to yell," I muttered.

"Well, actually," my father said. "Sometimes we do."

"Yelling is your father's normal voice," she reminded me. This is true. My father's idea of a whisper can be heard by people in several distant foreign countries.

"But think about it. We never call each other names. We never hit anybody or break anything," my mother said. "It doesn't happen that often, and when it does, it's just noise."

"No, it's not," I said. And I looked up at my dad. "It's really not."

"It's really not," Jesse said from the doorway, holding Sterling on his hip.

"Well," my mother said, patting my knee and standing up. "It's going to happen now and again. You'd think you'd trust us after twenty-three years."

"I'm only eighteen," I pointed out, sniffling.

"Fine," my father said, obviously thinking we were finished. "Eighteen years."

"Why did she leave?" I asked them.

My father sat down.

"We don't know, Nikki," he said after a minute. "It took us by surprise, too." He put his arm around me. "When you're young, you think love is one thing. And when it turns out to be harder than it looked, some people give up on it."

"Love is a nice feeling," my mom said. "But more importantly, it's a thing you have to do, even when you don't feel like it. I am not going to leave your father. Ever. He's too good a man. A lot of darned hard work some-times"—she batted her eyelashes too sweetly—"but ulti-mately, worth it."

"Sterling's getting cranky," Jesse said.

"Go put him to bed," my father told him, looking at my mother.

"Are we done, then?" Jesse asked.

"I think we're done," my father said, getting up.

"Except I never did get my point across," my mother said to my father.

"I'm sure you'll get back to it," my father answered grimly, taking Sterling out of Jesse's arms.

"You finished?" my mother asked me.

"I don't know," I said. "How can I believe you?"

She looked at me. Jesse was still in the doorway, but Dad had taken Sterling down the hall. "You'll just have to look at my life," she said. "That's the only proof I have."

It was not the easiest answer. But it helped.

She put her hand against my cheek. "I promise to do my best. I think you know I keep my word."

So that is what I am left with.

My life, hanging on their promise.

#9

Alicia

I have a plan.

Today was the first day that has felt like spring. I love it when the air gets soft and smells green. I hate spring rain. Such an anticlimax. But today, the sun was out for the first time in weeks. Now, you step outside, and the air slips across your skin like a soft blanket.

He was behind the school alone. I saw him when I was going to my locker during lunch; I just happened to look out the window at the sky. And he was there, smoking all alone, the thin line of gray from his cigarette drifting up till it just simply faded into nothing. His back was to the window.

It's an interesting feeling, knowing where he spends his lunch.

Sam

A week and a half. I have seen Jon seven times. I don't remember not knowing him.

I told my mom I was going there. She loved it. She told my dad I was doing volunteer work, so now I am on high moral ground. But he said, "You better get some experience handling money before you take off for college, is all." I can't argue the point.

Today, one of the inmates had a kind of fit. It really scared me. But one of the attendants told me what to do, and I helped. It worked out okay. It just weirded me out.

Then Tia made me read to Jon. Afterward, Jon smiled at me and patted me on the head and said I'd done a fine job. I felt really good about that. I guess I'm getting used to this stuff.

I look at those people, and I feel so sad. Jon is a person, the same as I am. He has a spirit inside, the same way I do. But he's trapped inside a damaged brain. I think about that, and it gives me claustrophobia.

It's not fair. Jon will never get to drive—never go to college, or read great books, or start a business. Why him and not me? Is it just chance? It makes me feel ashamed. Nothing in my religion tells me exactly why this is.

"Why don't I see your mom at that place sometimes?" I ask on the way home. Tia looks at me.

"Because she isn't there," she says.

I am praying for the day when Tia can answer a question without laying traps.

I just nod. I'm not going to leave myself open.

We drive along a little farther, and then Tia says, "My mom gave up on Jon a long time ago."

I glance at her, but she is not looking at me. She's just sitting there with the green seat belt holding her into the seat, looking out.

"You didn't," I say.

"No," she says. "I didn't."

She doesn't say anything else all the way home.

"Look," she says, when I have pulled in at the curb. "Let me guess: you have a big family and both of your parents are still in love with each other, right? They've been happily married for fifty years, and every one of the kids is above average."

"I have two sisters and a brother," I tell her. "I'm the oldest. My parents—my mother married my dad after my father left. About twelve years ago. But, yeah, I think they love each other. Is that what you want to know?"

She laughs to herself and looks away from me.

"And you probably all get along, right?" she asks me. "Like, your mother has your milk and cookies all ready when you get back from your hard day at school, and your father comes home and plays catch with you in the front yard every day. She wears pearls, and he wears a suit to work, and they always have time to talk to their little Boy Scout. And the family gathers around the table at dinner every night and talks about their day."

She is sneering.

"Why do you say this stuff to me?" I ask, suddenly really mad. "What, am I supposed to apologize to you that we all get along? Am I supposed to make you feel better by telling you that my dad and I yell at each other all the time?"

She whips her head around and burns me with a look. "Yeah," she says. She opens the door and she's out of the Jeep and up the walk. And I am just sitting there, wanting to hit something.

Nikki

I think it's going to work. What a relief. The four of us

spent three hours together in Brian's basement today, and nobody died. The hardest thing is that Kelly can't hold still and won't focus, so he isn't doing any of the work. I almost suggested he just bring his skateboard with him next time, so he could practice grinding on Camarga's front porch.

We have the site plan worked out now. Putting together a website turns out to be really fun. You have to make all the little maps so people can click, and then you have to plan the links.

We have a lot of the hard work done. There's still the text, and I'm a little worried about that. I know they're going to make me do it, and I'm not sure I can do it right. We want this to be cool but educational, so that kids can use it for research. We're even going to put a hit counter on it. I want to look at it a year from now and find out that a thousand kids have used it.

Stealing Brian Camarga was the best move I ever made.

Alicia

I can't sleep.

I've been sitting here in the window, trying to remember when this really started. There should have been signs all along.

I've been remembering a lot of things. The year we went to the mountains. Disneyland. Christmas. I remember when Ann was born. I just don't remember any ugliness. I thought she was happy. I thought we were all happy. Maybe I was just too young to understand. Maybe I just assumed, and never looked beyond that.

My memories are like home movies. I see Ann in her little jeans, ones I used to wear, running around the yard, looking for Easter eggs. I see my mother and me in the kitchen, making brownies for family night. All of us raking the leaves.

Peter keeps intruding into these pictures. I can't cut him out of them; he was there. He was always at our house. Peter and I used to dream that his parents would go away for good, and he could move in with us. It could have happened. His dad is a lawyer and his mom's a psychologist. They were always working, or off taking trips together. Peter had lots of nannies. He loved our family. He loved my mother. And I loved him. But that's an old story, and it's over now.

It's all over now.

Even school.

So many things that have defined me—being a daughter, being happy—the choir, the seminary council, the spirit committee. BYU is such a huge university—who will know me there? Will I even know myself?

I know I've had a wonderful life. At the same time, I feel like it was all a lie.

I am as lonely as the moon. As weightless.

From now on, I will have to make my own life.

I am nervous about tomorrow. I will find him in his hiding place. And he will speak to me.

#10

Nikki

Lunch. I might as well go to the library and get some sleep. Sam stares out the window. Alicia stares out the window. Peter gazes at Alicia from across the room. Nobody eats anything. Except me. I love to eat. And then, about five minutes after she sits down, Alicia gets up and leaves without a single word.

I tell you, it's creepy.

Alicia

I was very nervous.

I walked up behind him slowly. He was completely

alone, looking out at the trees. I could hardly breathe. I stopped about five feet away, and I looked back at the school nervously. But there was no one at the windows to see us. When I turned back, he was watching me.

My heart was beating so hard, I couldn't swallow.

"Hey," I said, trying to smile. I couldn't meet his eyes.

"Hey," he said, and turned away.

I came forward a step. "I was looking for you," I said, making my voice light and casual. He turned around and looked at me again. I walked closer, holding my books very tightly. That was a good thing; the pressure against my heart steadied me.

"Yeah?" he said, but not unkindly.

"I was thinking," I said, looking down, and then up—so difficult to look into his eyes—"that maybe we could talk?"

His eyes are so dark, you get lost in them easily. Dark and smooth and rich, and he uses them, steps behind them. I know this because now I've seen him do it.

"What would you want to talk to me about?" he asked. It was the first time I'd actually heard him speak. The real voice is the one you use when somebody is standing close to you, listening. He was talking to me as if I were someone small, somebody he didn't want to scare. And he was smiling a little. He looked down at his cigarette and then dropped it on the grass and stepped on it.

"I don't know," I said, because I really didn't. "I've just thought for a long time that maybe we should be friends."

He raised his eyebrows and nodded slowly. Then he looked away, his face toward the trees, and he grinned. The bell rang.

He glanced back at the school.

"You better take off," he said to me, gently. "You shouldn't be late."

"Okay," I said. I don't know what my face might have shown, but he studied it and then he smiled directly at me. A very private, unguarded smile. A smile that could slice your heart in half.

"Maybe sometime we'll talk," he said. "But now you better go."

So I gave him a little look—we've got a secret between us. I didn't even say good-bye. I just walked away, and I couldn't feel the ground. It was like I was wrapped in fleece, and it was incredible. For the first time in weeks, I felt completely alive.

Sam

I made a decision. I have to make limits. Tia is not my life.
Jon is not my life. I have AP's. I have a term paper. I can't
spend every day out at that place.

Nikki's after me: "Why are you mad?" She thinks I
hate her now. I haven't even talked to her for two weeks.
I can't. What could I tell her?

Not that it will matter to Tia. It's not like she thinks
that much of me.

So I didn't go to her locker today.

I went home. I studied. I started writing. All good
things.

Then why do I feel so bad?

Nikki

Today I worked with metaballs. Don't even ask what that
means—it would probably bore you to death if I told you.
It's a good thing I am developing new interests in my life;

I seem to have lost my good old friends.

My brother Jesse got his LDS mission call—two years in England—so the family went out to dinner tonight to celebrate. Then we went home and played bingo with M&M's as markers. Nobody ever wins when you play it that way.

I wish Alicia would talk to me.

I wish Sam would call.

Alicia

Nikki's parents argue. I've heard them. Sometimes you know they're really mad. That's when I leave. It's been like that since we were little. But you can tell they love each other. They all love each other at Nikki's.

My mother called tonight. My father stands holding the phone away from his ear, and I know it's her he's talking to. As if the things she is saying are too loud. I can't hear them myself, even when I am standing close by.

Even after she told him she was leaving, he loved her. It was like he loved her more then, because he was losing her.

I didn't blame her at first. I've been mad at my dad too, from time to time. Sometimes it seemed like he had to control everything. But I felt the same way about my mother.

When she left, my mother said she'd been living his life too long, and there was no way she was going to do it anymore.

I've heard my father say, "I know I've made mistakes." I've watched him try to fix things. He's always done dishes and laundry and cooking, but in the face of my mother's accusations, he started paying more attention, doing tons of work at home.

Before she left, he read books about relationships. He bought my mother flowers. He wrote my mother letters.

The flowers made her angry. I watched her read one of those letters, read and roll her eyes and then drop it in the trash. I pulled it out when she wasn't looking, and I read it myself. I would not have thrown that letter away, not ever in my life.

Then she left.

And one time, late at night when he thought we were asleep, I went into the kitchen for a drink, and I heard my father crying.

How can I forgive that?

#11

Nikki

Lunch, the third day this week. This is one for the history books. We had been sitting there at our zombie table for maybe ten minutes, when who should come waltzing up but Tia Terraletto?

Sam

I am sitting at the lunch table, punching holes in my milk carton. And suddenly, there's Tia.

Did I know she had first lunch? Have I ever seen her in here before?

She's walking down the aisle, looking somewhere

else, like she just happens to be passing by. Then she stops at our table. She doesn't bother to act surprised to see I am there. She knows I won't buy it.

She puts a couple of fingertips down on the table next to my lunch and leans over, driving nails into me with her eyes.

Nikki

Oooooozing up to our table. No. That's not right. She doesn't oooooze. She kind of—I don't know, how would you describe the way a cat walks? One paw placed carefully in front of the other, that aloof face, those wide eyes. She was even wearing a collar—a nice, black, studded collar. Which is a good design choice, because it tends to draw your eye up away from her legs.

She leans on the table and looks at Sam. "So," she says—

Sam

"I knew you'd bail." Her voice is low, but everybody at

the table can hear.

Of course, my face goes red.

"I didn't bail," I say.

She laughs and walks away.

"What was *that*?" Nikki says, watching The Walk as it moves down the aisle.

Nikki

But does Sammy answer me? Not really. He's too busy ogling Ms. Terraletto, all the way across the cafeteria and out.

Sam

"Nothing," I tell her finally.

I have just crushed my milk carton.

"*Really . . . ,*" Nikki says. Alicia says nothing. I look at her, but she is staring out the window. Nikki lets the word trail off, leaving little plumes of it in the air, like smoke.

"It's not what you think, anyway," I snap.

"And what do I think it is?" Nikki says.

Nikki

Defensive, isn't he? I make a small comment to that effect.

Sam

"Leave him alone," Alicia snaps. That takes us by surprise. But I can see Nikki gearing up, so I give in. I start to tell them—nothing personal about Tia. Not what she says to me—just basically about Jon.

What I don't say is "See—there's more to her than you thought." They are smart enough to get it by themselves.

Nikki looks thoughtful. Alicia has some other look on her face, like she just won an argument with Nikki.

"Tia's not the easiest person to get along with."

That much I'm willing to admit.

Alicia

It's hard not to slip out of here and happen by that window in the back of C hall. I find myself wondering why he goes back there. I would have expected him to spend lunch out in the west parking lot where the rest of his friends are.

But he doesn't.

He goes alone to the woods.

And when he is back there, what is he thinking?

Sam

Of course, I am at her locker that afternoon.

There's a little hitch in her walk when she sees me. Her face. It can't seem to settle into one look or another—and I don't understand any of them. I do understand the one she decides on, the mocking one.

"You're so predictable," she says.

"I'm not going with you today," I say.

She raises an eyebrow, but she doesn't look straight at me. She opens the locker and makes a big deal of messing with it. There isn't much hung on the inside of the door. A picture of Jon and of some rocker girl who looks like she could bite a metal bar in half.

"So?" she finally says.

"I can't go every day," I explain.

"So?" she says again, and she pulls out her coat.

"I just need you to understand that."

"Did I ask you to go every day?" she says. She flicks me with those eyes and turns to slam her locker door.

"No," I say. She is walking away.

"It's not because I don't want to," I say to her back. "I have responsibilities."

She waves a hand, but she doesn't turn around.

"Why don't you come with *me*?" I say, loud enough she can't pretend not to hear.

"Because I have to be at Jon's," she says, spinning around.

I am surprised. I have sisters. I know what it looks like when somebody's very carefully not crying.

"I can't just leave Jon for some—" She waves her hand, like she can't fill in the blank.

"Studying." I fill it for her.

She lets her breath out in a little huff, shaking her head. *I'm stupid* is what she's saying. "I have a life, too," I say. "Jon is your brother."

"Yes," she says, her face snapping shut. "He is."

And that's the end of it. She stalks off down the hall, and I can't think of another thing to say.

Nikki

I wrote a little HTML today. It was actually fun, especially when I got to see it turned into an actual webpage. Brian and Calvin are working hard to get this finished. They can be so completely focused—but they still helped me with the HTML. I worry about the text, but I don't want to bring it up, because the second I do, I know they are going to make me do it.

As I sat in Brian's room today, I suddenly realized where I was, who I was with. The most amazing thing was how at home I felt.

"People always talk about how rude the French are," my mother told me once. "But that's because so many Americans think the world starts and stops with them. America isn't normal. It's just America. There are a lot of wonderful normals out there—hang on to yours too hard, and you'll miss a lot."

I think I'm beginning to understand what she meant.

Sam

Two weeks since I remembered how to sleep.

I am getting no breaks at home.

I'm good with the little kids. I do dishes sometimes. I work hard in school. I live clean. Do I get credit for these things?

My life is measured in trash bags and gasoline.

I don't even cruise.

So now I am told: forget the trash one more time and the Jeep stays in the garage for a week.

I ask, how will I do my volunteer work, then? And my father says, "Take the bus."

Oh yes.

I wonder how it feels to flunk a history exam.

I think I'm going to find out.

#12

Sam

She will have to take the bus Saturday and Sunday.

She had to take it yesterday, and the day before.

That doesn't seem fair.

So I'm standing here now. To make it fair.

This time when she comes around the corner, she stops. For a minute, I think she's going to turn and go back the other way.

I don't move. When you try to get close to a wild animal, you have to be very still. I don't even look at her after the first shock. I pretend I don't know she's there. That way, she can make up her own mind.

Now she starts forward again. Now there is no Walk. She is moving carefully, almost quietly, the way you would if you didn't want to wake yourself. I have to look up after a minute. You can only pretend for so long.

At first, I don't say anything. But that feels wrong. So I say, "Hi."

She doesn't answer. The air around us feels like glass. Finally, she says, "Hi." Everything about her is shrugging, like she doesn't care if I'm there or not. I can see through that, and it scares me.

"I'm going out to Jon's," I say. "You want to ride with me?"

"I was going to take the bus," she says. I can see that she wants to go, but she's not going to say so.

"I'd like it if you came with me," I say. She glances at me, just for a moment.

She lifts a shoulder. "It doesn't matter. Whatever."

I push myself away from the locker. "Come on, then," I say. And we walk out to the parking lot.

"How was your studying?" she asks. Her voice is dull. She doesn't care; she's making herself ask. It's a step.

"I don't know," I say. "All I've got in my head is cognitive dissonance."

She looks up at me with this crooked grin. "Interesting," she says. "Cognitive dissonance. Do I get some credit for any of that?"

"You're the dissonance," I say. It's the first time I've felt like a player in whatever game this is.

"Good," she says, and looks down while she's walking, smiling to herself.

Now I'm really worried.

Alicia

My dreams are strange. I dream of Morgan. I dream of my mother. None of the dreams is easy. But not all of them were bad.

I made meat loaf last night. Mom used to let us choose dinner on our birthdays. I always chose meat loaf. Nikki laughs about that. "You should have gone for steak," she says. But meat loaf is my favorite. Especially the sweet sauce Mom used on top. I wonder what Peter's mother, the shrink, would say about that?

Mom didn't take her recipes with her. I guess I can assume that they are mine now. This is the first time I have made meat loaf myself. It was almost like some kind of ritual, a passing of power from my mother to me. Except she was not there to put it into my hand. My meat loaf tasted just as good as hers. But since she was not there to say no, I made myself twice as much sauce.

Peter keeps watching me. He does it at school, and he does it from across the street. If he wants something from me, he is too late. What little I have left is already taken.

Nikki

Here is an amazing thing: today, Calvin was complaining to me about how useless Kelly is. It was an us-and-them kind of conversation, and I was part of his *us*. I still don't like Calvin much, though. He and Brian are so different.

At lunch I told Sam and Alicia that Jonathan Hoffman asked me to the prom. "I turned him down, of course," I said. I expected at least a little sympathy from Alicia there. "I mean, obviously, I'm going to be spending the evening with Brian." I didn't say, *finishing up the project*. Not that it mattered; I doubt either of them were listening.

I think the whole Pygmalion thing has just kind of faded away. And that's ironic. Everything was fine until we made the pact. Since then, it's like all we ever were has faded with it. Now, I'm thinking Alicia never really chose anybody for it in the first place. And that's too bad—for both her and Peter.

Sam

It was good to be with Jon. She is always gentle when she is there. You forget the hair and the makeup and the dog-collar thing when you watch her with these people.

She is never gentle with me. Ironic, considering that she thinks I'm an idiot. I finally say this out loud. And she laughs.

"There are idiots who can't help it," she says, "and then there's the other kind."

"Maybe not," I tell her. "Maybe there's really only one kind."

But she doesn't like that. "Some people have choices," she says, and shuts me out for the next half hour.

She has the window open on the way home. It's cold, and I tell her so. She says she needs the air on her face. I pull up my collar and I don't say any more about it.

"Why did you come today?" she asks finally.

"I told you that I want to come," I said. "I just have other things, too."

She's quiet for a minute. Then she asks me, "Why do you want to come?"

Now it's my turn to laugh. "I don't know," I say. "Jon grows on you."

She nods slowly. "That he does," she says. She takes a deep breath, but says nothing more. Minutes pass.

"Really," she says finally. "Why do you come?"

I get a chill. I was getting used to the game. She's stepping out of that now. I'm not ready for her to do that.

"This is hard," I say finally. "You want me to be honest. But I can't. It's too hard when you mock me."

She looks offended. "I won't mock you," she says.

I give her this look: *I know you.*

She makes an exasperated sound, but the look she sends back is only half disgust; the other half is admitting I have a point. "I won't now," she says.

I laugh and shake my head.

"Answer," she says.

But it's too complex. Some things I cannot say out loud in front of her. The rest, I don't have words for.

"Why do you think?" I ask her.

But she doesn't buy that. "I'm asking you a question," she says. "I'm not interested in what I think."

"Because I want to," I say, finally. It's lame, but it's true.

"That's all?" she asks. "That's it?"

All I can do is shrug.

"So you're going to force me to ask you," she says. "You're going to watch me humiliate myself." As if it wasn't her turn. "Okay, fine," she says. "It's not because you like me, then."

I almost laugh, but I have just enough intelligence not to do it. "It's not like you make it easy," I say to her.

"Maybe," she says. She dips her hand into the wind. "But I don't think you hate me."

"No," I say, a little surprised.

"And you don't despise me," she says, like she's going down a checklist.

"No," I say again.

"But you don't especially like me, either," she concludes.

"Not true," I say. "I just said you make it hard sometimes."

"I make it hard," she says—with some pride—"all the time."

"Yes," I say. "That's precise."

She nods, seeming pleased. This doesn't feel like a game, but there are still rules here I do not understand.

"What do you hope to get out of this?" she asks me.

It's a question I have not anticipated. "What do you mean?" I ask, stalling for time. I am glad to see that we are close to her house.

"The question was clear," she says, sounding impatient.

"Maybe I don't think that far ahead," I say. Which could be true.

"I don't believe that. People who don't think that far ahead sleep better than you do."

"I never said I don't sleep," I say. I sound indignant, but really, I am surprised.

"Look at your face sometime," she says. I pull in at the curb. "Answer the question."

I sit there for a long minute. "If I try to put this into words," I say, "you have to promise that you won't rip on me."

"I can't promise," she says.

"Then I gotta go," I tell her.

"How about if I say I'll try my hardest?" she asks. "I mean it."

"How much effort have you ever put into 'trying' before this moment?" I ask her.

"Absolutely none," she says.

I nod.

Her face is way more open than usual. She is pretending to be casual about this, but I think she needs the truth.

So do I.

"Won't they worry that you're not home yet?" I glance up at the house.

She waves a hand. "Nobody home," she says.

So I take a breath. "I remember playing dodgeball with you a couple of times. Maybe you remember that? Out by the bars at Sunset View?"

"Not really," she says.

"Don't look at me like that," I warn her.

"Like what?" she says.

"Like I'm an idiot because I remember something like that."

She is surprised. "Sorry," she says. "I didn't know I was."

"You ought to look at your face sometime," I tell her. She laughs.

"Touché," she says. "Okay. I'll try harder."

I sigh and slide back into the seat. "You were always different, Tia. Even in junior high. You were like coals or something, quiet on the outside, but—"

"Hot on the inside," she guesses bitterly.

"There's all this stuff going on inside," I correct her. Very gently.

She searches my face. Then she turns away with an odd, still bitter smile.

"Is that enough?" I say, embarrassed.

"No," she says.

"I don't know exactly why I always noticed you," I say. Then I stop. I am now studying my steering wheel, running my fingertips along the bumps on the back. "So." I take a breath. "My friends and I decided we needed to get out of ourselves. That we needed to—choose somebody interesting and new and make a friendship." Too far from the truth.

I give the steering wheel a pat and make myself look at her. I don't even try to smile, because I just don't feel like it. She is still studying me. "So, " she says, "you chose me."

"Yeah."

She nods. "Interesting," she says. "So, is this a temporary thing? You score a friend, and then you go back to the way things were"—she opens her hands—"mission accomplished?"

"I don't know," I admit. "I didn't think it through that far."

"Because," she says, drawing out the word, "you know—friendship isn't—you don't get points for it and then the game is over."

"I know," I say.

"You can't just walk into a person's life and change things and then say, 'Thanks a lot. I'm done with you now.'"

"I know that," I say. Wondering if I do.

She looks up at the house. "Because," she says, still with her face turned, "I don't know if you've noticed, but it's not like I have a lot of friends."

I say nothing. She looks at me. "So," she says. And then she looks off again.

"You scare people away," I say, finally.

She nods. "I know," she says. And then she takes a very deep breath.

"This is very complicated," she says. And I immediately want to go home. All of a sudden, I'm terrified. Something in her face. Something in her voice.

"Is that what you want out of this?" she goes on. "To be my friend?"

I have to take my own deep breath, which I try to do very quietly. "Yes," I say, because it's true. But it's like giving my word, suddenly. Like signing a contract

I haven't read.

"You might want to think about that," she says, almost whispering.

She climbs back into the game face. She says, "We'll see, then. Since I know so much about your lovely family, maybe it's time I told you about mine.

"My mother," she starts out, and then she laughs, irony twisting the sound of it, "is what they like to call a free spirit." She does a little flourish with her hands to show me just exactly how free. "She went to college," she goes on, almost singing it, all fakey-light and quick, "and she had a great time, but she never did get her degree, because she had me. Because it's really hard to get a degree while you have to take care of a baby all by yourself. Which is what you have to do when the baby's father—assuming you know exactly which one he happens to be—isn't willing to stick around and help out.

"So, it's just Mom and me. Which is really fine by her. I mean, she was born to have a good time, and there were always boyfriends. Always a party. Then she meets Bradley, and I am about four or so, and Bradley is a real solid citizen. He owns a car dealership, and he has a house, and he has no kids, and he's pretty much tired of his wife. So my mother decides to marry him and settle down." Tia opens her hands: *so here we are.*

"A couple of years go by, and she has another kid. But there's a problem, because this kid comes out with Down's syndrome, which is a downer for Bradley, and for my mother, whose fault it evidently is. And there are fights about it. But they bring the baby home, and this is my little brother. So I do a lot of baby-sitting, which you may agree I seem to be pretty good at. And my mother gets a job.

"It works out, kind of, for the next three years or so, except there are always these little things that get in the way, like the school calling to find out why I miss entire weeks at a time. And my mother finally gets really tired of that, so she decides Jon would be much better off in a 'place,' which Bradley can certainly afford.

"And so Bradley puts Jon in a place where he's really *much* better off. And he probably is better off there." Tia looks toward the house again and stops for a second. She is taking long breaths.

I am listening.

"So, my mother went back to work. And I went back to school. And Bradley continued to sell a lot of cars.

There were fights about what the 'place' cost. He was always complaining that it wasn't worth the money. Telling her she didn't make enough to pay for the 'place' and whatever else she was spending all her own money on. He was supposed to be in charge of the family finances.

"My mother somehow always got him to keep paying for Jon. Big mystery, how. But the whole thing is getting to be this real drag on her, you know. I mean, you can understand that—having no control of her own money, and then there are these kids, and the shame of having one that's retarded—the poor woman.

"And this husband who just keeps getting fatter and balder, blackmailing her about money, giving her grief over what time she gets home, who she's e-mailing—and after a while, there came a point when she was sick of the weight. It was 'holding her back.' And heaven *knows*, if there had ever been any mystical kind of love between her and Bradley, it had long ago evaporated." Tia looks at me.

"So she left," I guessed. I thought about my dad leaving and knew it was not the same thing.

"Yeah," Tia says to me. "She did. She just took off one day while I was at school. She left a note: have a nice life, kid. Fun knowing you. She didn't even leave a note for Jon, but then, she never went to see him anyway. I couldn't even go visit him myself till after I got old enough to figure out how to read a bus schedule.

"For a while, I just got up in the morning, got ready for school—and I made breakfast for Bradley every day. I was about twelve then, almost thirteen. I was making dinner, too—but I'd been doing that for a long time anyway, since I was the only one who wasn't working.

"And then, one day, Bradley told me he wasn't going to pay for Jon anymore. That the state could just come and get him and do whatever, he didn't care. I cried, and I begged." She shrugs. "It didn't matter to him. And then—then, he made me a deal. He said that he'd been pretty well ripped off by my mother, leading him on and then sticking him with these problems. He said he hadn't gotten much satisfaction out of the whole deal. But he said—hey—mother, daughter, didn't make that much difference to him, as long as there was dinner on the table and his other needs were looked after. He said, if I wanted to see things that way, I could keep living in his house, and he'd take care of Jon."

She sighs. And then she looks at me.

I am trying to hold my face still.

"What was I going to do? I could have taken care of myself. I could have made it on the street if I had to"—this came out way too lightly—"but Jon . . . I couldn't do that to Jon."

I let go of my breath. She does that terrible, ironic little laugh again. "I don't have a lot of time for friends," she says. And then she goes ahead and tells me the kinds of things that have gone on in that house, and when she is finished, I am shaking.

"It's all right, Boy Scout," she whispers. "But this sure makes everything different, doesn't it?"

I can't even open my mouth to lie to her.

"Don't faint," she says, not quite mocking.

"You have to consider a little bit before you decide to be friends with something like that," she tells me. "Anybody would." She opens the door and begins to climb out of the Jeep.

"It doesn't matter," I say to her, but I choke on the words. She gives me a reproachful look and starts up the walk. I can't say anything. I can't call her back. I just sit there, staring at nothing. There are tears running down into my mouth.

I hear her front door close. And after a while, I start up the Jeep and drive away. I get as far as the park on Center before I have to pull over, and then I barely make it to the trash can before I lose everything.

#13

Alicia

I know that I am not going to make it to the prom. I don't have enough time left. I've only spoken to him twice. I actually suspect he is not and maybe never will be the prom type. The conventional type. The rent-a-tux-and-buy-flowers type.

But this was never about the prom. It was about giving somebody a chance. About believing in him. It was about never breaking faith with hope.

I'll tell you what Morgan is: he is the highwayman type, the man in the dark mask and the rippling cape who scales the wall to leave a rose on the sill at midnight. He is the type who hides a heart wound behind a laugh but would kiss a woman on the palm before he left her.

He is the type who, once understood, is a private world of quiet intensity, who walks the night for its treasures and avoids the gaudy light of day. He is the kind of man a woman would die to love.

I half expect to see him under my window tonight. But the moon is almost gone, and the shadows are too deep for me to tell.

Sam

I didn't take out the trash; the entire universe will collapse.

We shouted. I threw something. I don't even remember what. It shattered.

But I didn't storm out of the house. Where would I go?

You can turn off the lights. You can climb into your bed. But you can't turn off your mind. You can't stop the pictures.

You can't sleep when it's your soul that's nauseated.

You can never sleep again.

Nikki

Nobody understands how I feel about this project. My parents listen very patiently when I talk to them about it. But I know they don't really understand what's happening to me because of this. I worked on it so hard this week and talked about it so much Saturday, my parents finally ordered me out of the house. "Away," they said. "Go away and find something nonproductive to do."

Sam

My mother wants to know if I'm sick. My dad says, if I'm not, there's lots of work to do around here. So I just do the work.

Nikki

I called Sam, thinking we could go bowling or something. But he wasn't interested. "I have chores," he said. I tried to jolly him up a little bit, begging and wheedling, but he stonewalled me. Almost like I was some stranger. The only thing I can figure is that I've done some stupid thing and made him mad.

So I've been trying to figure out why. It's hard to pinpoint *exactly* why, since I'm almost always in trouble for something, somewhere. It could be because I still don't like Tia very much.

I thought about calling Alicia. The truth is, talking to Alicia has gotten too hard.

I had a history test to study for and another paper due in English, and I still had to do the lab sheets for zoo. But how boring. It was Saturday. I needed something happy. Like my mother said, something nonproductive.

I just sat there alone on the front porch, watching cars go by. Then Jesse came out and flopped down beside me. "Not much kickin'?" he said. I shook my head.

"Tell you what," he said. "Let's get the kids and go skating."

First I was going to say no. When you're getting depressed, nothing sounds good. But he stuck me with his elbow and did Groucho eyebrows at me and got me to laugh.

"Then we can go to a movie," he said.

I grinned at him. "What's bringing this on?" I asked him.

He got thoughtful. "Two years away from you guys is a long time," he said. "Got to have something to remember you by."

And he even bought us burgers.

Sam

My mom wants us to play miniature golf this afternoon. "I'm sick of chores," she says. Everybody else in the family starts dancing around with joy. My dad points out that it's chilly for miniature golf. He also points out that it's Saturday, which means crowds.

My mother laughs. "You gotta take some chances in life," she says.

Neither of them like it when I say I don't feel like going. My dad starts gearing up to go head-to-head with me about something he really doesn't want to do either. Then my mother moves between us and starts making these silly mommy eyes at me.

Of course, I go.

And in the end, it helps. My littlest sister is fierce about doing stuff herself, and she's so terrible at golf, it really is funny. My brother hits all the water traps; my mother's freaking because he's getting his feet wet. The wind is blowing, and we are freezing the whole time. So being here has made me laugh, made me feel annoyed about being so cold.

But nothing can save me for long.

I am going to carry this horror for the rest of my life.

Alicia

I took Ann with me to the mall today. She's growing so fast. Last week at church, she was complaining about her Sunday shoes, how they were too tight. That's one of the things I remember about my childhood: Sunday shoes are always too tight.

So we went to Penney's and got Ann some new ones. Some late Easter shoes. That's another thing I will remember, my mother taking me shopping for Easter shoes.

Sam

I don't feel like going to church. But I feel less like arguing. So I put on my suit, and I go.

I am sitting in the pew with my family. The meeting is going. I look at my sisters and my father, and suddenly, I don't want to think of them at the same time.

I can't sing the hymn. Singing takes something I don't have right now. But I am listening.

I am not asking myself why God lets these things happen. I think I understand the answer to that. The way I see it, God puts us here so we can make our own choices. He can't keep things like this from happening unless he takes the right to choose away.

No, the question in my mind right now is how does God, who loves us, watch all of these terrible things and not die? Not just die of the sorrow?

I never knew what horror meant before. I wish I didn't know now. They are saying the opening prayer up on the stand, but I don't hear the words; I just hear myself, deep in this black pit, screaming. And I am screaming, *why.* How could people do these things? It's people I'm terrified of. I never knew that anybody real could ever, ever, ever let themselves choose such horrible, horrible things.

So I am saying, *help me, help me,* over and over. My mind is like some kind of bird with no feet that just has to keep flying around. But really, I think I mean, *help her, help her.* Or maybe I mean *change the world; I don't want any more choices.*

I can't take the sacrament. I hold too much of the horror inside of me.

My mother is looking at me now, but I can't help that. I can't do what I can't do.

Time goes on. After a while, I am looking at the people who are sitting around me in the chapel. I have known them all my life. Part of me wonders what things their lives hide, how much I always thought I knew, but didn't. Then something takes my thinking, the way my mother takes my face in her hands. *Look,* it says. And I look again.

I remember what I said to Tia about the coals, how she reminded me of a coal. There are not a lot of people in this room who remind me of coals. I know that there are problems here: Mark Evens has to be on medication, and Glen Bartalamous, my old Scout leader, is gone from home so much, it makes his wife unhappy. I am aware of these things. My parents are aware of them.

There's probably a lot of stuff we don't know, too. But this is a whole room full of people, and I honestly don't believe there could be many stories here that come anywhere close to Tia's.

When I think that, I look at my dad. It's then that I remember: every day I see how he treats my sisters. I watch how he treats my mother. I live with his choices. And I realize that I don't have to be afraid of him. There is nothing horrible about my dad. In fact, I know he is good. Suddenly, I feel this wash of love for him. This terrible wash of longing. And I am crying, and I cannot stay in the room.

It doesn't matter that I have to climb over people. It doesn't matter that they see me crying—I can't stay in there. I get to the front doors, and I am out of there, and heading down the sidewalk.

I can't slow down when somebody calls my name. I just keep moving. But it is my dad, and he catches up to me. He puts his hand on my arm, and I turn right into him, and I am sobbing into his shoulder. I don't even care.

I just don't even care.

Alicia

And where is God in all of this inequality? In mothers who leave their children and children who have nightmares? Why is one born in a house with parents who do nothing, or worse than nothing, while another is brought up by hand? In the end, are we judged as if life were some kind of race—you only win if you successfully make it to the finish line? How fair is that when some people had to start miles behind the others? Shouldn't the finish line change for each person?

My mother, in the end, decided that she could not believe in what she called "your father's church." I sat in the pew with Ann and Daddy today and I listened dully to the words. But I do not think I can follow Mother where she has gone. The words still make sense to me, and I know that I will keep believing them. I just wish that I was still one of the ones who are confident of blessing, one of the ones whose good lives seem to get good results.

But most of all, I wish she were here again with us, and this terrible time was all over.

Sam

I told him.

I told him the whole thing, right from the beginning.

We missed the rest of church and walked all the way home. On the way we ended up sitting in the park for a long time.

I felt so tired.

And he listened.

"Man," was all he said.

Telling him was like throwing up when you're sick. It all comes up and out, and it's not all inside you anymore. Except I'm afraid that you never actually get something like this out.

At least for that moment, I didn't have to hold it by myself.

"So," my dad says finally. "What are you going to do about it?"

This was not what I was expecting to hear.

"What do you mean?" I ask him. Suddenly, I am feeling the old defensive anger. "What am I supposed to do?"

"You're going to have to tell somebody," he says. "You can't know this and not take some kind of action."

Which is again not what I want to hear.

"This is pretty horrifying," he says softly. "It makes you wish you could just go over there and kill the guy." He looks at me. "But you can't."

Frankly, the thought hadn't even crossed my mind. "I

can't talk about this," I point out. "It's not my business." But that came out wrong. "I don't mean—I mean, she confided in me, Dad. She didn't open up to me so I'd go around telling people."

"You sure about that?" he asks me. Which makes me mad.

"Well, what do you think?" I ask him.

"I think that sometimes people say things out loud when they are ready for help." He is looking down at his hands.

I just shake my head. Now I feel even sicker. "This is way more than I know how to deal with."

"Me too," he says. "But you can't leave her there. And it doesn't matter whether you tell me and I report it, or if you're the one who blows the whistle, Sam. You're going to catch it either way. It seems to me, if you're really going to be her friend, you can't let this go on. And there's not a whole lot you can do about it personally."

"We could let her come live with us," I heard myself saying. But that scared me almost worse than anything else.

My father didn't answer right away. "I think," he started slowly, "that wouldn't be real fair to your mother. She's pretty much got her hands full with you kids. To bring something like that into the house—she's the one who would have to deal with it. I'm not sure she's got the tools for it, Sam. If that were the only solution, we'd have to do it. But I don't think it'd be good for anybody concerned. Or wise, considering the relationship between you two."

I was so relieved when he said that, it made me ashamed.

"This is why she didn't believe I meant it. When I said I wanted to be her friend." I had my hands pressed tight between my knees. "I'm not that good a friend, am I? Only up to a point."

"Friends look out for each other," my dad tells me. "Sometimes it isn't easy."

"So what do you want me to do?" I ask him.

He sighs. "Man," he says again. "I think maybe you tell the school counselor. Seems to me, that's the best way to handle it. Is there one you think you can trust with this?"

One.

"Yeah," I say.

"It's a good place to start," he says. "But I wouldn't discuss it with anybody else." Which brings up another worry: Alicia and Nikki watched me barge out of that meeting today.

"I don't want to do this," I say. He laughs and gives

me a one-armed hug.

"I know," he says. "I wouldn't either."

Nikki

Something is happening. This morning at church, Sam got up in the middle of the meeting and practically sprinted out of the chapel. I wasn't close enough to see, but somebody told me he looked like he was crying.

This makes me feel sick.

Sam

I am lying here in the dark. My eyes won't close.

And where is she?

That's easy. In hell.

She tells me all this stuff, and then I don't call her.

But I've never called her.

What if I call her and that guy answers?

No. I'll just meet her at her locker.

She has to be wondering. But only till tomorrow afternoon.

Then she'll see me there and know I didn't give up
on her.

But it's what she doesn't know that will be making
me sick.

#14

Nikki

Oh, Sam. I thought you were mad at me. Now I know it's not my fault. Nothing I do is that important. Not enough to make you cry.

And *I* thought it was all about me.

I am a lousy, lousy friend.

Sam

I am terrified that Tia will show up at lunch.

I can't eat. Nikki is pretending not to notice me. Alicia hasn't noticed me for weeks. This should be a comfort. But it's not. I know they saw me at church. Nikki isn't

145

asking me about it. This is unnatural. But then, I left natural behind weeks ago.

"I want you to do me a favor," I tell them anyway. "I
just wish you wouldn't ask me."

"Ask you what?" Alicia says.

Nikki looks at me for a long time. "Okay," she says.

Nikki

As if I would ask him. At least he's still speaking to me—
or to us, anyway. Maybe we can build on this—even
though we aren't talking about the elephant in the room,
we have to try to talk about something.

Sam

Nikki looks at Alicia. Alicia doesn't notice. Nikki's face
gets tight, and she shakes her head. "Sam," she says very
seriously, "you have to think up some topic we can discuss."

So I think for a moment. I bring up the genome work
sheet. Nikki looks relieved. And we talk about that. At

least, Nikki and I do. Alicia is lost in her own head.

It's hard for me to keep track of our talking. I am too worried about seeing Ms. Hyde. About what I am about to do to Tia. How do I talk to her before I do it? How will I ever talk to her again after?

Nikki

The genome assignment. Very safe. Alicia didn't even bother to pretend she was listening. So we did talk—a little. At the end, the conversation didn't really die so much as just fade away.

After about three minutes of silence, Alicia said—very politely—she had to go. And I don't think Sam, who hadn't eaten a bite of his lunch, even noticed she was gone. He just sat there, poking absently at his plate.

Alicia

I had to do something. When I hold still, I think, and if I let myself think, I'll start screaming. I couldn't just sit at lunch, listening to people talk about genomes. So I left. I went out to the woods.

He wasn't there. But there was always the chance that he would come. So I sat down on the grass, and I tried very hard to study, and I waited.

The sun is new these days, and the baby leaves are a brilliant, vibrant green. You notice these things when you are trying to distract yourself. This afternoon the sky was robin egg blue, and the air was a little breezy, but the new sun achieved a friendly warmth, especially when the wind dipped for a moment, which it does not yet often do. I had to keep sweeping my hair out of my eyes.

I didn't hear him come. I don't know how long he had been standing there. When I looked at him, he was watching me. He wasn't smiling. Then he walked over and looked down at me. I couldn't breathe.

"Hi," I said to him. I was trying to seem serene and graceful, but I think my nerves took my voice up a little too high. With horror, I realized that I had just sounded perky. I was embarrassed. He laughed.

"What are you doing out here, princess, freezing your whatever off?"

He did not say "whatever," but I didn't care. My mother used to have little names for me, "honey" and "baby," things like that. But no boy has ever called me anything special before. Princess, he said. I felt my face go hot, and I looked down, trying not to grin.

Then I realized I hadn't answered him. I just held up the book. He nodded and smiled one of those secret smiles of his. I suspected that he knew very well I'd come out there to find him. And it seemed he didn't mind it at all.

His eyes were gentle. His soul in his eyes, real behind a mask.

"At least come back here around the corner," he said. "Out of the wind, for whatever's sake."

So I got up and he helped me pick up my notebook, and I followed him around the corner, where there's a little retaining wall. The second we got around there, we were out of the wind. The sun was much warmer, the bricks of the wall radiating like tiny furnaces.

He sat down with his back to the heat and looked up at me, one eye screwed up against the sunlight. "Are you going to sit?" he asked.

I sat on the ground next to him, even though there wasn't any grass there. I was strangely calm.

"So," he said. "What did you want to talk to me about?"

I'd worked through the words a thousand times. I

needed to be open, but not pushy. I longed for him to see me for what I really am, so that he could let me see him. But it was hard to start.

He closed his eyes and put his head back against the bricks.

"I just wanted to say . . . ," I started, my voice trailing off. I threw my hair back over my shoulder and looked out through the trees. "I suspect," I began, "that a lot of people don't really see you very clearly."

He didn't say anything, and I couldn't bring myself to look at him.

"I believe," I went on, "that there's way more to you than anybody knows." I glanced at him then.

He was nodding, very slowly. Thoughtfully.

"I just wanted you to know that I believe that. And—if you ever feel like you need to talk to somebody, or if you ever need a friend, I'm here. That's all."

He did that little private smile again, and then he looked at me. Honestly, it was almost too big to hold, the feeling I got when we looked straight into each other's eyes. He smiled again, but this time it was a full, honest smile. I got chills all the way down my arms to the tips of my fingers.

I wanted to reach out, to touch his hair, to brush it

out of his eyes. But I didn't dare.

"Hey," he said, nodding again. "That's cool. I don't hear whatever like that very often."

"I just want you to know that somebody cares about you," I said, and now I was nodding, too.

Then he said, very gravely, "Thank you." He hunched up his shoulders. "But it's getting a little cold out here." He stood up and offered me his hand. I put my hand into his, and he pulled me up easily. He smelled like cigarette smoke. Even so, I was looking up at him, and the moment had a clear, crystalline quality to it.

"You better get your book," he said.

"Oh," I said. I had to turn around and bend over to get it, and I nearly fell over. The moment was gone. And then the bell rang.

"Another time," he said, connecting again with his eyes.

"Another time," I said. And then I had to wait a few moments, standing there, freezing in the wind until he'd had time to make a decent exit.

I know what he's generally supposed to be. But I also know that his real life is only beginning.

Nikki

Peter caught up with me again today. For a moment, I thought he wasn't going to say anything. We just walked along together, silently down the hall. Then, without turning to look at me, he said, "She's in trouble, you know."

I didn't answer.

"Nikki," he said, "I'd give anything to be in your position with her right now. Then maybe I could do something."

When I finally glanced over at him, he was gone. I turned, walking backward, and watched him disappear into the crowd. That was when I finally started realizing I'd been avoiding Alicia emotionally. Putting her off in little ways.

One thing I was sure of—Alicia could have chosen more wisely all those years ago; Peter would never have been scared to be her best friend.

#15

Sam

Is she ever going to come?

Yes. She comes, and we are back to the beginning; she's bright and hard, and she acts like she doesn't see me standing there.

"Can I go with you today?" I ask her.

"Suit yourself," she says.

Once we get to the place, she seems better. It's my fault that she is this way. My fault she doesn't know I am still beside her. If she is afraid I see her differently now, she is right. I am only a kid. She is something other than that. Before, she was a mystery. Now, she is a screaming demonstration of the fact that there are edges you can fall off in the universe. She is a refugee, one hundred years old. She is not a girl you casually take to the movies.

I read to Jon. She reads to Jon. Jon pats her. "You're smiling a lot," he says to her. He doesn't seem happy about it. He doesn't want her to go when we are finished. "You can stay," he says.

By this time, she seems a little more relaxed. She can't quite look me in the eye, but she has lost that brittle flash.

We walk out of the place together, talking about Jon.

We get into the Jeep, and she says, very casually, "I didn't think you'd be back."

"You never think I'm going to be back," I tell her.

She makes a little laugh. "Fair enough," she says. But I have not said the right thing yet.

I don't start the Jeep. We are not looking at each other.

"I can't tell you that it doesn't matter," I say finally. "But I'm here today. Same reasons as before."

She nods. When she looks at me, I can see she is once more near crying. But Tia doesn't cry. I am learning that.

"Good," she says. But she adds, "You can't come every day," like she's reminding me. I don't know what I am supposed to say after that.

I start the Jeep.

She is silent all the way home. Her face is turned away from me, into the wind from the open window. I try to focus on my driving. We pull up in front of the house—that house she should never go into again. She turns to me.

I don't know this look. I don't know what it means.

She leans forward and takes hold of the front of my jacket. The look is deeper. She pulls me toward her. And then she kisses me.

It is not like a girl's kiss. Not like the girls I know. It is something else. Everything ignites. It goes on and on until I have no breath left to breathe. Until my hands are full of her hair.

When it is over, I can't speak. I am shivering.

"I want you to come inside," she says. "Come into my house."

It's like lightning, the shock that runs through me.

"I want you to," she whispers.

She takes my hand, and I feel like I am made of electrified water.

I say, "I thought you said forget it." My mouth is completely dry.

"That was before," she says softly, touching my face.

"That was when it was what *you* wanted. Now it's about what *I* want."

"I can't," I say. She is pulling me, gently, insistently, toward her again.

"Yes, you can," she whispers. "Yes, Sam—because I need you to."

But I can't. I can't. I have never felt like this in my life, and I never knew I could feel like this. Every part of me is on fire. She no longer has to pull on me. But part of my brain is still functioning, remembering: I have made this very decision in my head a thousand times before now. If I do not hold on to that, I will no longer be myself—even if I'm holding just by my fingernails.

I have to pull myself away from her, reversing this engine that's driving me, backing away—and I do it very, very gently for both our sakes. It's not what she expects. It's hard. And as she realizes that I'm serious, her face begins to change.

"Why not?" she asks, before she closes on herself again. Before she stops speaking the truth.

"I don't," I said. "I'm just—I just won't. Not till later."

"What do you mean, 'later?'" she asks. The edge is coming back into her voice.

"In my life," I say. Our eyes are locked together;

there's a beam going from inside of her to inside of me.

"You're kidding me," she's saying. Like, how could I turn this down? How could I push her out?

"Tia, why are you doing this to yourself?" I ask. "This should be the last thing you want."

"Should be?" she says. She straightens up, and the beam is broken. I have said something very wrong. "Fine," she says. She gathers up her stuff.

"No, wait," I say. Things are happening too fast.

"Forget it," she says, and then says something very rude.

"I wanted to ask you," I say, talking fast, trying to get it in before she gets away entirely, "if you want, we could do something tonight or tomorrow. Maybe we could get Alicia and Nikki, and we could—"

She turns on me, her eyes blazing. "You think I want to go 'do something' with you and your little friends? You think I want to be anywhere near those *girls* of yours?" I know the look she's wearing now. The one that says I'm a total idiot. She is gone from me. Severed.

She throws one hand up.

"Good-bye, Sam," she says. "Have a good life."

She is out of the car. She is done with me.

I sit in the Jeep for a long time, my forehead resting

on the steering wheel. I'm still breathing hard. It's a long time before my hands stop shaking. I have two pictures running in my head—of her in the Jeep just now, of her having to live in that house. I keep trying to shove them out of my head; together, they make me completely sick.

But no matter how long I sit there, no matter how long I wait, the feeling of that kiss on my mouth will not go away.

When I get home, my mother says to me, "Did you do it?"

"No," I say, shocked at the question.

"You didn't talk to the counselor? Sam!"

All I can do is stare at her. "I couldn't," I finally say. "I couldn't." And shame washes over me.

I can't eat dinner. I can't stand the way they are looking at me. So I excuse myself, and I go to bed.

Tomorrow. Tomorrow I will go to Ms. Hyde.

Nikki

Best friends.

I'm supposed to be Alicia's. But I'm scared to talk to her. And I'm supposed to be Sam's—ditto. The things that are going on in their lives are too big for me. Life used to be so simple, and I can't figure out how it changed.

I snapped at everybody in my family all through dinner.

What a swell person I am.

I have nothing but contempt for people who run away. For people who desert their friends. Therefore, after dinner, I had a choice: to not be that kind of person, or to live forever in shame and self-contempt. So I called Alicia. It was not easy. Just waiting for an answer made my hands shake.

Ann answered the phone.

"Hey," I said to her.

"I'll get her," Ann said.

"Hello," Alicia said. Not "Hi," not "Hey."

"What's going on?" I asked her, not sure whether to support her by being cheerful and optimistic, or by being sympathetic and sad.

"Just the same old," she said. She sounded tired.

"I don't think so," I said. "These days, nothing feels the same."

"Yeah," she said, her voice going edgy, "well, that's because it's not."

"No," I said carefully. "It's not."

"No," she said. "It's not." She was quiet for a moment.

"Some things are," I said. "Like you and me."

"You," she said. "Not me."

"Are you different?" I asked her. She laughed.

"I am so old," she said. "I am older than I ever wanted to be."

"I'm sorry, Alicia," I said. "I am so sorry."

"Nikki," she said, "I used to come home and tell my mom about my day. I think about that now, just 'Blah, blah, blah.' Happy, 'Blah, blah.' If somebody had told me, you only get your mother for another three months, you think I would have wasted it like that?

"And now—there's no dinner unless I do it. There's no laundry unless I do it. Ann won't get home unless I pick her up. My dad tries, but he can't leave work early all the time. I can't take anything for granted anymore, Nikki. Even my dad is different. I think I know more about him now than I ever wanted to. And I'll tell you what: if the sun doesn't come up tomorrow, I don't think I'll be all that shocked."

"Oh, Alicia," I said lamely. "This is terrible."

"Oh. No. That isn't the terrible part. This is the terrible part: last night, my mother's ex-best friend told us—that L.A. publisher my mom was working with? He just filed to divorce his wife."

"Oh," I said. I pressed my hand over my stomach and

sat down on the bed.

"Yeah," she said. And then she laughed a little. "You know, I really thought, if Daddy didn't sign those papers, somehow, it would all work out. I just thought—but now, I've lost her. Completely lost her. Like, she's not even the person I thought she was."

And then neither of us had anything to say.

Then, "Alicia," I said desperately. "Maybe we should just go and do something fun tonight. You want to maybe go see a movie? Or get some pizza?"

I heard her take a breath. "I can't, Nikki," she said. "I've got to be here for Dad and Ann. This is really hard on my dad." Her voice broke.

"I'm sorry," I whispered.

"It was a good idea," she said. "I just—can't."

"Okay," I said. "I'm sorry, Alicia. I'm sorry."

She took another breath. I heard her let it out. "Well," she said. "I've got to go finish the dinner. I'll call you later," she said. "Love you."

"Love you," I said. But it left a bitter taste in my mouth.

I hate her mother.

I looked at my family tonight, and I thought about what her mother had thrown away.

I hate her mother.

Sam

I don't understand. She doesn't even know me. She doesn't know that I don't know how to handle money. She only suspects that I pitch fits when I'm wrong. She thinks I'm a Boy Scout. She's never heard me yell at my family.

Why would she want to be that close to me?

Why would she want to belong to me?

Or would it have been the other way around?

I wonder if she knows how perilously close I came today to forgetting everything that has ever been important to me. I could have lost everything, the respect of my family, my future, the self I thought I was.

The blindness only lasted a second. But that it could happen at all—there's the shock.

So, now I know another new thing about myself.

#16

Sam

If I hadn't gone first thing, I wouldn't have gone.

I spent the whole night praying about it. I know I have to do this. I know it's right. But my hands are still shaking.

Ms. Hyde is young and pretty. I sit down in her office, and I feel light-headed. I explain that what I am about to tell her is hard to say because it is really not my business. I tell her that I think a friend of mine is in bad trouble.

She's good, Ms. Hyde. She tells me that she admires somebody who has the courage to do what I am doing. I feel even more ashamed; I am not brave. I just feel like throwing up. But she keeps talking, and it makes me feel a little better, a little safer.

Then she scares me. She says that, if what I tell her concerns the safety or abuse of myself or of any other person, she has to pass the information on to the proper authorities. But that it is already too late for me to turn back. She explains, the moment you know something of this significance about somebody, it is your moral obligation to act. If you do not, then you are actually partly responsible for whatever harm ends up coming to that person.

I cannot even feel my hands anymore. How do you put words to these things without choking on them? I stall, explaining, "She told me these things privately. I am breaking her trust."

Ms. Hyde does not see it that way. People speak what they want somebody else to know.

Couldn't it be, I ask, more about testing me? About wanting to know how much of a friend I really am?

Ms. Hyde says this could be so. "And that is why you are doing this. Because you are a good friend."

So I take a breath and I start. I do not look at Ms. Hyde. I keep my eyes on my hands, her desk. Some of the things are very hard to say. When I finish, Ms. Hyde sits back in her chair and is quiet.

She says, finally, "If the situation truly is as you have

described it to me, then Mr. Terraletto—"

"Mr. Bendelow," I correct her. "Tia doesn't have the same name."

"Mr. Bendelow," she resumes, "is committing a crime against a child." She explains that she's going to call in Officer Rowland, who is the cop assigned to our school, and give him the information. She asks if I would be willing to talk to the officer. And I think, *why not?* Anyway, I know his kids. He's a good guy.

I have to wait for him.

Luckily, once he gets there, Ms. Hyde tells him most of it. She just wants me there to make sure she gets it straight. I make corrections here and there, which calms me down a little. When they are finished, Officer Rowland turns to me and explains that they are going to have to call Tia out of class and talk this over with her. He asks me to wait in another room in case they need me for any reason. They are very kind to me.

I feel like somebody has poured chemicals into my blood. I have never felt nerves like this, not even before a state championship game. My eyes are hot. My hands are cold. I take my backpack with me and sit down where they tell me, and I try to do some studying. I can't even focus on the page.

I am imagining how bitter she is going to be. I have betrayed her trust. I know she will be humiliated. I know I have done a terrible thing. Terrible but right. It's not supposed to be that way. You're supposed to feel good when you've done something right.

I wait a long time. Inside my heart, I am hoping that they never call me, that this thing with Tia will just go away, that Tia will just go away. But only part of me feels this.

When the officer does come for me, I almost ask him if I can stop in the bathroom for a moment. In the end, I don't ask.

I walk into the room, and the only thing I see is Tia. She is sitting on the hard chair against the wall. She looks cold and dark as obsidian. When I walk in, she only glances at me, and the look scorches.

"Would you like to reconsider what you've just told us?" Officer Rowland says to her.

"Do you want to explain where you get off telling this crap about me?" she says. Her voice is sharp as a knife. "You must have some serious problems."

"You're saying then, that none of the things Sam told us are true?" the officer asks.

"I'm saying that—," Tia begins, and then she describes

me. She is using her ripest vocabulary, all at once. Basically, what she is saying is that I have made these things up to make trouble for her because she denied me sex. I feel like somebody has hit me hard in the face.

It all sounds very convincing. Now I am getting the cold feeling that what she told me was maybe not true after all. Maybe she lies all the time. How would I know? But I think of how she is with Jon, and I can't believe that.

"All right," the officer says gently. "Let me explain what will happen next. Because this report has been made, and the offense indicated is a criminal offense, an investigation will have to be conducted."

Tia opens her mouth to speak, but he puts up his hand. "Tia," he says. "We never take any chances when one of our kids' safety is in question. An officer will be going to your house tonight to talk to your stepfather about this."

Tia's eyes become huge, and her face goes white. "Fine," she says. "Go talk to him. It's all lies; what's the difference?"

The officer continues patiently, "What I need to know now is if you feel comfortable going home, knowing that this is going to happen."

"You don't have to send anybody," Tia says. "I don't even know when he'll be home."

"Someone will be going to your house tonight," Officer Rowland says firmly. "If they can't find him at home, they'll find him at work." Tia's breathing is faster now. "Do you feel that you will be safe at home tonight, if that happens?"

"Please leave it alone," she says. And then she looks at me. "I can't believe you did this to me," she says, her voice throaty with anger, her eyes no more than slits. I don't say anything. "You can't have somebody talk to him," she says to Officer Rowland. "You don't understand the situation."

"Then maybe you can explain it to me," the officer suggests.

She raises her hands, as if she is holding something in them. "You can't—," she says. "It's too—" And then she puts a hand against her mouth, and the hand is shaking. She takes the hand down and folds it with the other in her lap. "My brother," she says. "I can't . . ." But she doesn't finish. "Please don't do this," she says to Officer Rowland. She is trying to be very reasonable. "You don't know what it will do to us."

"Tia," Officer Rowland says kindly, "it's out of your hands."

Suddenly, Tia's face begins to crumble. She covers it with both palms. We all wait. Ms. Hyde puts one hand on Tia's shoulder, and I am surprised that Tia doesn't shove it away. Then Ms. Hyde has both of her hands on Tia's shoulders.

"What am I going to do?" Tia asks. The iron is gone from her voice. "How am I going to take care of my brother?"

"We'll work it out," Ms. Hyde says. "We're not going to let anything happen to him. Right now, we're far more concerned about your situation, Tia. I have to ask you again: did Sam tell us the truth?" This time, Tia throws her hands up and turns her face away from everybody. Then she nods. "You have been very wrongly used, Tia," Ms. Hyde says to her. "And it's time somebody looked after you.

"Sam," Ms. Hyde says. "You need to go back to class."

"I want to go home," I tell her.

"Will there be someone at home when you get there?" she asks me.

"Yes," I say.

"Then go on into the outer office, and I'll get you excused," she says.

Tia looks up at me. "I want you dead, Boy Scout," she says.

"So, I was just supposed to leave you there," I say to her. I am having trouble swallowing. "Is that what you wanted, Tia? For him to keep hurting you?"

"There are a lot of ways to hurt somebody," she says to me. Then, through closed teeth, "This was my life. My choice. At least it was my choice." She turns her face away.

Ms. Hyde follows me out of her office and closes the door. "You can't live Tia's life for her, Sam," she says. "But you did the right thing."

Nikki

Sam wasn't at school. How could I help but wonder why?

I talked to Alicia a little. I informed her that I am already conceding Pygmalion defeat. "I never had time to work on changing him," I said.

"What matters," she told me, "is that you didn't just slap a label on him and write him off. You have to give a person a chance to be what he is."

"Yeah," I said. "And I think maybe Brian already was what he is."

She blinked at me. Then she looked up at the clock.

"Gotta go," she said, apologetically.

"Why?" I asked her.

"I need to drop by the library," she said, but the way she said it, I knew she was lying. So there's more going on with Alicia than the stuff at home.

"Okay," I said, but not like it was.

"Call you later," she said, and went off, weaving her way between the tables to the door.

"Yeah," I muttered, and glared down at the rest of my lonely lunch.

Alicia

He didn't come.

I went out there and I waited.

I kept thinking it didn't feel right. That it was an anticlimax, me looking for him, after yesterday. I suspected that it was supposed to be his turn, that I should be waiting for him to come looking for me.

I didn't sit down. I turned around to leave twice. I guess I couldn't let go of hoping he'd be glad to see me.

Finally, I got too uncomfortable. I was sure that if he ever did come, my being here would ruin everything.

Once the thought took root in my mind, I was terrified that it was already too late, that he'd show up before I could get away.

I left quickly, dodging back in through the door with my eyes down, just in case.

Luckily, it was in time.

So I never did see him.

I am so glad I didn't make that mistake.

Sam

I am not going home. I want to see Jon before this is all over. So I drive to Spring City. It is the first time I have been there by myself. When I walk in, the woman at the front desk says, "Hey, Sam, aren't you a little early today? And where's Tia?"

I say, "Tia's in trouble. I don't know if she's going to be able to come in today. I don't even know if she will ever go home again." These people really care about her. That's always been obvious. From the way they look at each other now, I get the impression they are not that surprised. Maybe even that they are relieved.

"What happens to Jon," I ask them, and this is one of

the reasons I have come, "if Tia can't pay the rent?"

The lady gives me this weird look. "What rent?" she asks me.

"For this," I say, waving at the building.

"There isn't any rent," she says. "This is a state institution. Nobody ever paid any rent for Jon."

"What?" I say. I have had too many shocks.

"No rent," she repeats.

I let go of my breath. I am thinking about Mr. Bendelow, and I am using words in my head I would never allow to come out of my mouth. And now I am trying to figure out how to tell Tia this, so she won't worry. Like she ever wants to hear from me again.

"Can I go up?" I ask her.

"Not now," she says. "Jon's in class."

I nod.

"But you can leave him a message," she says helpfully. She gives me paper and a pen. I draw him a picture, a sky with mountains and a tree, and I write: "To Jon from your friend Sam." And I leave it.

I will try to find Ms. Hyde's number tonight. She will tell Tia. Then at least Tia will be able to sleep.

Nikki

Wonders never cease. By yesterday, we were done with all the graphics, all the links. We were very close to being finished with this whole huge project. "What we need now," Brian announced this afternoon, "is the text."

Brian and Calvin turned to look at me.

Then Kelly said, "I'm on it." He dug a folder out of his backpack and presented it to Brian.

Brian pushed his glasses up his nose and opened the folder. We all sat there, watching as he read. He started nodding. "This is good," he said, sounding mildly shocked. "This," he announced a moment later, "is perfect." He shoved his glasses up again and peered at Kelly.

"You wrote this?" he asked.

"Sure," Kelly said. "It's not like I had anything else to do."

"Brilliant," Brian concluded.

So there it was. Kelly had worked the whole thing out, frame by frame. Brian immediately got to work, entering the text and putting the fades in so that the words came up along with the rest of the animation.

"Well," Calvin said. "This has put us ahead of schedule.

Tomorrow we can *upload*." And then we all started to yell and dance around.

I was hugging everybody.

Who woulda thought?

#17

Sam

I tell my mother everything. I know my father has already told her everything. But I need to say it all over again, to put it into a story, a clean little package I can store away in my head.

I still can't eat anything without losing it. So I decide to go to bed.

"I'm worried about you," my mother says.

I can't help her with that.

Alicia

We're poor. My mother divided up all our stuff. She let

my father keep the house and one of the cars, but only if he refinances and gives her half the money. He could have gotten a lawyer. He could have fought it. But why? What would be the point? Our lives have already been destroyed; this is just one more thing.

Can you really do that with your life? Divide it neatly in half?

Anyway, now it's over. She's gone. Now we have a house and a car, but no money. I wasn't supposed to know this.

But you know what? She's not going to beat us. She betrayed him. She betrayed Ann and me. She still calls and wants me to talk to her. But you know, trust is a fragile thing. It doesn't just break; it shatters. I'll talk to her, but it's going to be a long time before I ever again say anything. It's hard to put something back together once it's in tiny little shards.

So she may have taken the money, but my father is a hard worker. We won't want for anything. And I don't mind cooking and buying stuff with coupons. We'll make it. We'll have to be careful, but we'll do fine. I will make sure of that.

I feel strong now. Very strong.

Nikki

I waited for Alicia to call me after dinner. Finally, I gave up and called her. When she answered the phone, at first I wasn't sure who I was talking to. This voice belonged to the old Alicia, the one I used to know.

"How's it going?" I asked her, not daring to hope that her family troubles had just suddenly up and vanished.

"Just great," she said, which was obviously patently untrue. "How did the project go this afternoon?"

"Great," I said. "It turns out that Kelly Smythe is a brilliant writer."

"Kelly *Smythe*?" she said.

"Yeah. How's that for a surprise? You just never know, do you?" At least I don't. These days, I'm fairly sure I don't know anything about anything.

"Well, that's great," she said. "I can't wait to see it."

Uh-huh. "So," I probed, keeping my voice light, "what great thing happened to you today?"

"What do you mean?" she said.

"Alicia. For days, you've been lying on the floor with ashes all over your head, and suddenly, you sound like a mother cat in a box full of kittens. Something happened today."

There was silence. Silences have begun to scare me.

"Nothing happened today," she said, suddenly grounded. "You know, life is so ironic. Just when it's the worst, you can feel the strongest. We know where we stand with my mother now. We're moving forward. We're going to make our own future. I feel very determined about this. Very *firm*.

"And, Nikki—there is one bright little spot in my life right now. It's very delicate, and I don't want to talk about it. Except that I really do want to talk about it. So I will tell you, but only if you promise you'll listen with an open heart. Okay?"

"Okay," I said, just as cautiously.

"Because this is important to me. Seriously."

"Okay," I said again.

"It's about Pygmalion," she said.

Ah. Finally, secrets of the ages, revealed.

"I finally got him to talk to me," she said.

"Who?" I asked her.

"Morgan," she said.

"Morgan?" I echoed stupidly. At first, absolutely nobody came to mind. Then an ugly picture popped into my head: "Morgan Weiss?"

"It wasn't easy," she agreed.

"What do you mean, you got him to talk to you?" I asked, trying to keep my voice level.

"Well, actually, it was more like *I* talked to *him*—but it wasn't me completely," she said, sounding very happy. She was using that dreamy voice, that visionary one, and it scared me to death. But I was inside her guard now, and I was going to have to be very, very careful if I wanted to stay there.

She went on. "I know how he seems on the outside, Nikki. But it's so misleading. There's far more to Morgan than any of us know."

"What did you say to him?" I asked her, hugging myself.

"Just . . ." She trailed off. "Let's just say I left the door open."

"I didn't know you had any classes with him," I said, very casually.

"It was when I left lunch early the other day," she said. "I kind of ran into him out behind the school."

"Behind the school?" I echoed. "You were out by the woods?"

"He always goes there during lunch," she explained. "But it's just by the building on the grass. Not *in* the woods."

"It's off-limits back there. You never go back there, Alicia," I reminded her. "You can't just 'run into' people out there if you don't ever go there yourself." My voice was rising—I couldn't stop it.

"You do if you want to talk to somebody who's there," she said, starting to sound a little ruffled.

"Okay. I just want to understand this. You left lunch early, and you went out by the woods with Morgan Weiss and his friends?"

"Not with his friends," she said, like how could I think she would be so stupid? "He just goes out there alone," she explained, that dreamy tone in her voice again. "Doesn't that tell you something? His friends are always out in the west parking lot, smoking. And he goes to the woods, alone."

"So, you were alone by the woods with Morgan Weiss. Alicia—why would you ever be alone by the woods with Morgan Weiss?"

Long pause.

"Because I chose him, Nikki. Just like you chose Brian Camarga."

"But Morgan—," I started.

"You know," she said, "this is what I was afraid of. You're so rigid the way you look at people. I knew you would never understand."

"Alicia," I said. "Wait. Okay, then you've got to explain it to me. You chose Morgan Weiss, who has actually been arrested, who has a reputation that would scare a junkyard dog. You meet him alone by the woods. But you won't even talk to Peter. I thought you'd choose Peter. If anybody's ready for a little redemption, it's Peter."

"I don't want to have anything to do with Peter," she said angrily.

"Why do you hate him so much?" I asked her. "He's cute, he's kind, and he cares about you. I don't understand this."

"That's because it's none of your business," she said. "You know, Nikki, I've got an English paper to do."

"So do I," I told her. "Look, whatever Peter did, it can't be half as terrible as the smallest, least threatening thing Morgan Weiss does. You won't give Peter a break, but you give Morgan Weiss a break?"

"You know what?" she said. "I'm not going to explain this to you. I'm hanging up."

"Alicia, you've got to answer this one."

"Say good-bye, Nikki," she said.

"You're scaring me," I told her. "I don't think you're seeing very clearly."

"Talk to you later," she said, her voice all fakey-light, and she hung up.

I was left with the dead phone against my ear and an awful sense of foreboding.

Alicia

She never really gave him a chance. She never really tried to know him. She only saw what she decided was there. Never looked beyond that, not in all those years. How can anybody do that, write a person off without ever trying to understand him?

Obviously, all along, the only person she ever cared about was herself, and since she had to convince herself that she was the innocent victim, she protected herself with lies. Just lies and whining.

I'm glad she's gone. I don't think I've ever really hated anybody in my whole life till now.

I just wish I could stop dreaming about her.

#18

Sam

My brain is trapped.

All night long, I couldn't turn it off. I couldn't lie still. I couldn't find peace.

And I'm sure I must be sick.

I am not going to school today.

The sun comes up. It doesn't make any difference. My mother sits on my bed, looking down at me. "You better talk," she says.

I tell her I can't. But then I do. And I keep talking, like I can't stop.

My mother runs her fingers lightly through my hair, the way she does when I am sick.

"Sam," she says, "you are not a bad person because

you have a good life. It isn't bad or irresponsible to be happy. There's a lot of unhappiness in the world—but just because you're happy, that doesn't mean you're cheating.

"This life of yours didn't come free, remember. It's the result of generations of choices and work and teaching. My folks got it from their folks and then passed it on to me. I made some unwise choices," she goes on, looking away. "I was lucky—I got you kids, and I got a second chance. Since then, I've respected the gifts—the work ethic, the values, the faith, the self-discipline—they handed on to me. And the gratitude. You know what would really be bad? If you were ashamed of this gift so many people passed on to you—ashamed instead of grateful and determined."

"But," I tell her, holding my stomach, "I don't deserve it."

She laughs. "Who does?" she asks. Then she gets serious. "Spend your life making everything you touch more beautiful and peaceful and healthy for other people. That's how you end up deserving it. The trick here is to tell the difference between what you can fix, and what you can't. Or shouldn't."

She yawns and stands up. She pulls the covers up

and tucks them under my chin. "Sleep as much as you need to today," she says. "But life begins again tomorrow, and I'll want you out of here."

Nikki

This was the second day Sam wasn't at school. So maybe he's just sick after all. Alicia came to school, but not to lunch. So there I was, alone at our table, feeling like this giant neon arrow was hanging from the ceiling, pointing right at the top of my head.

Finally, I got up and went over to sit with Brian and Calvin. It was the most socially fulfilling lunch I'd had in weeks. At least they carry on an intelligent conversation half the time.

I left lunch—in the middle of a discussion about some anime series—and went hunting. It's risky to wander the halls at lunch; if they catch you, you get detention, no questions asked. So there I was, sneaking down one hall, peeking around the corner, ducking into the girls' room in C. I don't know how Alicia does this; she's not the sneaking type.

When I got to the place where the doors open out on

the forbidden back lawn, I plastered my face against the glass, straining my eyes back and forth, scanning for Alicia. The lawn was deserted. I was not completely reassured; there was always the chance she had already been dragged off into the woods.

I dropped by her class at the beginning of sixth period, and of course, there was Alicia, sitting in chem like it was the normalest thing in the world. And of course, I got a tardy off Mr. Webb.

After school, I went to Brian's for the last time. Everything was finished. There was a moment of tension when Brian and Calvin got territorial about whose website was going to host the project. But that passed, and our pages went up on the Net without a hitch.

"We're done," Kelly said happily, as Brian clicked through the links.

"So it seems," Brian said.

"So, we could still make the tournament," Calvin said, his face glowing.

"Tournament?" Kelly asked, sounding interested.

"Majik," Calvin said, in his you-wouldn't-understand voice. Kelly shrugged. "Whatever," he said.

We all looked at one another. Finished. No more meetings after school. No more working together. It should have felt like a relief, but nobody seemed all that relieved.

"I guess I'll see you guys around," Calvin said. Slowly, he packed up his stuff. "Need a ride?" he asked Kelly.

I was the last to leave. I picked up my backpack and looked at Brian. "I want to apologize to you," I said. "I shouldn't have butted into your partnership with Calvin."

He swiveled around in the chair. He pushed his glasses up and made that snorty sound. "So you're sorry you did the project?"

"No," I said vehemently. "I loved doing the project."

"Fine, then," he said. "Don't be sorry you butted in. I'm not sorry. In fact, if you want, you could come over sometimes, and we can work on modeling." He swiveled back to his screen.

"I'm glad you get to go to your tournament," I told him, swinging my backpack up onto my shoulder.

"Now you can go to your dance," he said.

And wasn't that sad?

I called Alicia after dinner.

"I looked for you during lunch today," I told her. "You weren't out back."

"No," she said. Her voice was cold.

"So where were you?" I asked her. I was friendly and supportive.

"You wouldn't be interested," she said.

"Sure I would," I told her. "Did you find Morgan?" I dangled the name in front of her, figuring it would warm her right up.

"Yes," she said, but reluctantly.

"And what did you do?" I asked.

"Took a walk," she said.

"Where?" I asked her.

"It doesn't really matter, does it?" she said to me.

"So," I said, forging ahead, "was it nice?"

"Yes," she said.

"And what did you talk about?" I asked her.

"Nikki," she said, "you don't want to know. You just want me to tell so you can lecture me."

"No," I lied. "I'm just wondering what Morgan Weiss talks about." Murder? Anarchy? Hot-wiring Camaros?

"I did most of the talking," she said.

"And you talked about . . . ," I prompted.

"Just stuff," she said. "About how we all have gifts from God so we can make the world better."

"Really," I said. "And what did he say?"

"He was very kind," she said.

"But what did he say?" I asked again.

"Nikki—," she started.

"Alicia," I interrupted. "I'm just asking. How will I ever understand if you don't tell me about it?"

I heard her sigh. "He said—he calls me 'princess,' Nikki. Nobody's ever treated me like that, so don't say anything to wreck it. He said, 'Princess, you're a nice girl. You shouldn't be out here with me. But you've been nice to me.' And then he got very serious, and he took my hands, and he looked me straight in the eyes. 'I'm going to give you some advice,' he said. 'I think you better stay away from me. I'm not good for you.'"

I swallowed.

"And I said, 'Morgan, I want you to understand that I trust you.' And he got very intense, and he said, 'Don't do that. Princess, that's the last thing you ever want to do.'" She stopped.

"Wow," I said.

"So, you see what I mean?" she asked.

"I see that he has a very strong point," I said.

"No. A bad person would never say something like that. A bad person would just take advantage of you. That was honor, Nikki. He is an honorable person. He just needs somebody to believe in him."

"Alicia," I said, "I think you better take him seriously."

"I am," she said.

"No," I said. "I think you better listen to him."

"You're judging again," she said.

"Look," I said. "I know you aren't supposed to judge. But you only have so much you can give. If you're going to bankrupt yourself, you want to do it where it's actually going to make some kind of difference in the end."

"Nikki," she said, "I think it's time to butt out."

And that was the end of that conversation.

I had to call Sam. Whatever else had been going on lately, this really did scare me. And I couldn't handle it alone.

"Alicia's in trouble," I told him. "I know you've been mad at me about Tia—"

"I'm not," he said.

"Maybe not anymore, but you were in the beginning," I told him.

"Not everything's about you," he said to me.

"See," I said. "You're just biting my head off."

"No, I'm not," he said.

"Well, what do you call it?" I asked him.

"I'm not mad at you, okay?" he roared. "So just leave it alone, okay?"

I just love it when he gets Neanderthal.

"What about Alicia?" he asked me. And I suppose *that* was supposed to be a completely pleasant tone of voice.

"Oh, nothing," I told him. "It just that she's been stalking Morgan Weiss. Sam—she's in love with Morgan Weiss."

"Morgan Weiss," he said.

"And not just from afar. She's been *talking* to him. She's taking *walks* with him. She's meeting him in the woods. Sam, she thinks he has a *soul*."

"Most people do," Sam observed.

"That's not the point," I told him. "You know Alicia. She thinks he's drowning, and she's the only person in the world who can save him."

"What if she's right?" he said.

"Sam," I yelled, "he's bigger than she is. And when she's like this, she doesn't see straight. Okay, he may be in the water, but—it's like an ice rescue: the only way you're going to save anybody is to make sure you stay on the solid part—you lie down, and you put your hands out, and they have to grab on and pull themselves up, or else you both go through."

He took a deep breath.

"She believes in fairy tales, Sam. She believes in *Beauty and the Beast*. She believes in Tam Linn. She believes in closet character. The thing she doesn't believe in is ice."

"So, you want to haul her back on the bank," he said.

"Yes. Exactly. The question is, how? Her family's messed up. You're messed up. She's mad at me. We have to get back to normal here."

He was quiet for a minute. "You could be right," he said, and he sighed. "So I should probably call her. Maybe we could do something on Friday night. You want to do something Friday?"

"Yes, I want to do something," I told him. "I *long* to do something normal."

So I left it all to him. I don't know, maybe Sam will sound so melancholy, she'll switch to wanting to mother him.

#19

Sam

I have to see Ms. Hyde. There are things I need to know. So I go to her office before school. She looks up from her work when I knock on the door. "How are you doing?" she asks. The question means something when she asks it.

What can I tell her? "I'm dealing with it," I say, as if this whole thing had been about me.

But I'm supposed to work on not being ashamed.

I explain that I want to know what has happened to Tia.

Ms. Hyde tells me that Child Protective Services came to get Tia that day, right after our meeting. The only other thing she could tell me was that Tia had gotten my message about the rent. I asked Ms. Hyde if she could find out more. She said she would make some calls.

"Sam," she says as I start to leave. I wait. She goes on, "If Tia makes it through this—and I'm warning you, it'll be tough—it'll be Jon that saved her. The things she's done for Jon. That she loved him that much. But it will take time. You've got to give her time."

As if I have anything to do with this anymore.

Alicia

I am ice.

I am dead.

My face doesn't move.

I walked my customary way this morning, and there was the usual mob at the corner. I looked for Morgan. I knew he would not say anything to me in front of them.

When I saw him, my heart quickened, and I felt every single atom in my soul.

And then I saw more clearly, and that is when it all shattered.

There was a girl with him. No, not with him—*on* him, *around* him, *fused* to him. She was tall and she was built like—I am fighting metaphors, ugly, bitter metaphors. He had one arm around her, his hand—but it doesn't matter where his hand was. She was plastered against him, laughing, and he was looking at her face like it was something he wanted to eat.

I know that girl. And you know the ugliest irony of all? Her name is also Alicia.

There was one second, just one second before I had passed him entirely, when he looked up and saw me. And our eyes met.

And now I know why he did this.

He is trying to hurt me.

He is trying to drive me away.

He is trying to save me from himself.

Nikki

"I talked to Alicia," Sam told me.

We were sitting at our lunch table with Rob and Matt and Mikey and Judd and Kirk, who were busy making up a script for their parody of *The Scarlet Letter*.

"I didn't talk about Morgan. Just about tomorrow night. She wants to go." Sam kept watching the lunchroom door. "She's not going to make it to lunch, is she?" he asked.

So we ate a little and then went hunting for her. We nearly got nailed in C hall. We checked the back—nobody there. Checked the west parking lot. Got to the library just as the bell rang. And there was Alicia, writing poetry.

Sam

I'm driving out to Spring City again today. Funny. I'm not sure why I am doing this. When I get there, I end up reading Jon two books. It's weird to be there without Tia, but Jon and I do okay. The ladies are nice to me.

I am relieved that there is no rent here. I had been thinking about getting a job to help with that. It's a relief I don't have to.

Nikki

I don't think I ever actually understood the magnificence of RNA until we did this project. There's a magic about taking something apart, drawing it, rebuilding it—after you do that, the thing becomes yours in a new way. Now, when I think about these complex processes that go on in our bodies millions of times in the blink of an eye, I am full of awe. It's so beautiful.

I found our site today with my own computer. All over the world, anybody with a computer can get to it and see our names as the designers. It is the most significant thing I've ever done.

Alicia

I told my dad I was going out tomorrow night with Sam and Nikki. It's silly, I guess, but I was excited about getting pizza and seeing a movie and just hanging out.

Then Ann said that Rachel had asked her over for a sleepover.

And here's the really funny part: I was just feeling sad and guilty that I was going out to have fun while my father sat home all alone, when he said, "This is actually going to work out very well, because I have a date myself."

"I have a date," he says. Like it's perfectly all right to drop something like that without even leading up to it.

Without ever clueing us in on this as a possibility in his life.

"You remember Holly," he says to me.

And I want to shout, "What are you talking about? I don't remember any women."

And he goes on to talk about how they'd been good friends in high school, and how he'd just run into her the other day at the Home Depot and found out that she's alone in her life, too.

The thing I don't understand is, I thought we were doing just fine. I thought he was so torn up. I thought it would take him a little time, at least, to get over the complete ruin of his family. I thought I'd been taking care of things for him.

But I guess I wasn't good enough.

Did he ask us if we were ready for something like this?

Did he ever stop to think about that?

Evidently not.

#20

Alicia

I broke the silence. I said his name in front of all of his friends and made him come out to me. And I told him I had to go with him tonight—it didn't matter where, but I had to go. He tried to put me off, but I begged, and I did not let go of his eyes.

He said he'd think about it.

I could feel their eyes on my back, all the way down the hall.

Sam

Ms. Hyde says that Tia is in a group home. Vantage Point.

I'm not sure what this means. I do know that it means she will be safe. And they will have counselors for her, if she will use them. Ms. Hyde says that Tia can stay there, probably till school is out. After that, she can be a legal adult. On her own. When that happens, Child Services may help her out with her rent and utilities for a little while.

Today was the first time in weeks I have gotten anything out of my classes. It's going to take time for me to get used to being normal again. In some ways, these classes—AP history, zoo—seem a little trivial now. But I guess you need different perspectives in your life.

I'm going to have to study hard these last weeks. No matter what my dad may say about how I don't need grades, he'll kill me if I walk through the door with a handful of C's.

It will feel good to do something easy tonight. Fun to see a movie and mess around with Nikki and Alicia. Like the old days. When we were kids.

Nikki

It was going to be so simple. Sam, Alicia, me—out on the

town. How hard could that be?

First Sam calls and tells me he has to baby-sit. "Didn't you tell them we had plans?" I whined. "Didn't you tell them it was *important*?"

But when have parents ever been moved by such arguments?

"I can come late," he told me. "I hope not *really* late."

"Fine," I sneered. "Alicia and I will do each other's fingernails till you show up."

Little did I know.

It was just getting dark as I drove up Alicia's street. There was a muscle car at the curb in front of her house. The rear passenger door of that thing slammed shut as I pulled in behind, and then the car took off, screaming down the street.

"What was that?" I murmured, squinting at the back of it. Then I looked up at Alicia's house. The porch light was on, but there weren't any other signs of life. I narrowed my eyes, scanning for the taillights of that car, but they were long gone. Robbers? Murderers?

"Man," I muttered, getting out of my car. "I hope not." That's when I nearly fainted. There was this guy standing on the sidewalk across the street, staring at me. At least, he seemed to be staring; it was getting too dark to see.

"Nikki," the guy said.

"Who is that?" I asked, groping behind me for the door handle.

"Peter." He started across the street toward me. "Who did you think?"

Massive relief. "I don't know," I said. "Whose car was that?"

He leaned back against my car. "Morgan Weiss was driving it," he told me. He didn't sound happy.

"What?" I said. I turned around and looked up at Alicia's house.

"She's not home," Peter said. "Didn't you see her get in that car?"

"What?" I shouted. "You let her get into a car with Morgan Weiss? Why didn't you stop her?"

Peter laughed.

"Where's her father?" I demanded. "Why isn't he doing something?"

"Not home, either," Peter said sadly. "Nobody's home. Not there"—he waved at Alicia's—"not across the street" —he waved at his own house. "Nowhere. Just me. And evidently, these days, I'm lower on the food chain than Morgan Weiss."

"Let's call your father, then," I said, too frantic to

be thinking straight.

"Why? He's just a lawyer. Anyway, my parents are on a cruise," Peter said. "Like I said—nobody home but me."

"On a cruise? Without you?"

"I didn't want to go," he said. "I had school."

"We were supposed to go out," I said, staring down the street. I was starting to get mad now. "The least she could have done is called. Called and told me she was dumping me for a homicidal maniac. Why couldn't she have at least *called*?"

"Wouldn't know," Peter said. "Persona non grata, remember?"

"Will you stop whining?" I said, turning on him. "If you don't like the way things are, why don't you do something? You sit around, watching her from afar and sighing. You're so tragic, Peter."

"Well, what am I supposed to do?" he asked, and now he was angry too. "I've apologized. I've groveled. I've brought flowers and had them thrown in my face. When we were thirteen, I even offered her my damn bike. She hates me, Nikki. She hates me forever. And where am I? You want tragedy? I'm in exile, that's where. I loved her mother too, you know. But do I get to grieve? Do I get any comfort? No. I'm just the sick jerk across the street."

That stopped me. "Peter," I said. "Just exactly what was it you did to her?"

"It's too stupid," he said, and he pushed himself away from my car. I took hold of his arm.

"I am so bored with secrets—so bored. Just tell me, Peter. What kind of betrayal can you do when you're twelve years old?"

He let his breath go through his teeth, and he sagged back against the car. "You want to know?" he said. "Fine. You see that window up there? The one right above the front door? That's my room." He was pointing to his house. "If you look closely, you can see that it's directly in line with that window, right there." Now he was pointing at Alicia's window.

"One time, Alicia and I ran a string all the way across the street from her window to my window—you know, with cans. Like a telephone. That's how straight across those windows are from each other."

He shook his head and sighed. "In the summer, when the air was real soft, we used to have this flashlight code we did after we were supposed to be in bed."

"And?" I prompted.

He shifted, looking down at me. "Alicia's right. You're a pain."

"Oh, thanks," I said. A car went by, then another. I kept hoping it would be her dad.

"You remember in seventh grade, Mrs. Williams gave us that bird list?" he went on. "My dad got me these binoculars so I could do the bird list. He told me, if I got all twenty, he'd give me a bike."

"The one you tried to give Alicia?" I asked him.

"The very one. Well, one day I was up in my room, and I caught this flash of wings in the tree over there. So I grabbed the binoculars, and I was focusing them, trying to find that bird, when my eyes kind of"—he swung his hand through the air—"passed right across Alicia's window."

"So?" I said.

"I guess she must have been just getting out of the shower or something. Whatever, she was standing right in front of the window . . ."

"Oh no," I said.

"Well, she wasn't completely . . . ," he said. "But enough. And I thought, Whoa. What did I just see? And you know, I should have just put the binoculars down, right then. But I didn't."

"You *looked*," I said.

"Yeah," he said. "I looked. Only for a second. Well,

maybe longer than, like, *one* second. And then the sun must have reflected off the lenses or something. Anyway, she caught me.

"That look on her face—right in my binoculars. Man, she saw me, and then the curtains came down, and that was it. The end of everything."

He blew his breath out. "So. Now you know. The next time I saw her, she called me a pervert. And that's the last thing she ever voluntarily said to me."

"Peter," I said. "She was your best friend. You were a Peeping Tom. That was sick."

"No, it wasn't," he said firmly. "It was a perfectly normal thing for a twelve-year-old boy—well, for a guy of any age, actually—to feel like doing." He shrugged. "It's just 'normal' and 'right' aren't that synonymous all that often."

I made a disgusted hiss.

"Look, I learned my lesson, okay?" he said. "I was wrong, inconsiderate, shallow—all those things. I messed with her privacy and reduced her to nothing but a body. I know. I understand completely.

"But I still don't think it's right for somebody to be condemned forever because of a mistake they made when they were twelve. It's not like I'd ever do anything like that again. I learned, okay?"

He made an exasperated noise and shook his head. "Just one stupid mistake. I was a kid; how did I know it would end up mattering so much?"

"Poor, idiot Peter," I said. Then, "You're absolutely sure you wouldn't do it again?"

"Absolutely," he said—with passion. Then, "At least ninety-nine percent. So now she's off with Al Capone, and I'm standing in the street."

"What can we do?" I muttered, trying to think. "Why don't we go look for her?"

Peter shook his head. "Where would we look?" But when I opened the door of my car, he started around to get in the other side.

Another car was coming.

"Wait," Peter said.

The car passed under a streetlight and pulled into Alicia's driveway. "Enter: the cavalry." Peter laughed, starting up Alicia's front walk. Alicia's dad got out of his car, walked around to the far side, and opened the passenger door. We heard laughing, and then he and a woman I didn't know came around the front of the car and on across the lawn.

"Looks like we have company," I heard Alicia's father

say. "Who is it? Nikki? Alicia said you were coming over tonight. Why are you standing out here? Come on in." He held something up in the air, sounding very happy. "We have pie."

#21

Nikki

We followed Alicia's dad and his friend into the house.

"Nikki, this is Holly Bizzell," he called from the kitchen. The cute-looking woman with dark hair smiled at us and gave us a half salute. She was wearing jeans and a nice sweater. "Holly," he said, coming back into the living room, "this is Nikki, Alicia's friend, and—ah. Peter. I thought you were Sam. Peter. Good to see you." This last, he said with a mixture of complete sincerity and apprehension. Then he walked over to the stairs. "Alicia," he called.

"She's not here," Peter said. "And we need to talk to you about that."

Sam

I am being very patient. I clean up the supper. I clean up the kids. I play Candyland. I play Sorry. I read stories. I get no studying done.

My parents come home an hour late. I don't even complain. They hand me the keys, and I finally get to drive over to Alicia's. It's now so late, I don't expect to find anybody there.

What I do find is total bedlam.

Alicia has lost it. What is she thinking? What kind of a girl gets into a car with somebody who does the trash Morgan Weiss does?

Peter is there, which just adds to the weirdness. But he is the calmest person in the house. He and this lady friend of Alicia's dad. The rest of them are freaking out. But nobody's actually doing anything. Myself, I'd like to get out there and cruise until I find those guys. It wouldn't hurt my feelings at this point to be banging some heads.

Nikki

Alicia's father kept standing up and sitting down, running his hand through what hair he has left. We were all huddled around in the living room, trying to figure out what to do.

"Do you have any baseball bats?" Sam asked. Alicia's father actually took the question seriously.

"Why don't we call the police?" I suggested.

"And tell them what?" Peter asked.

"That a really nice girl lost her mind and voluntarily went off with a gang of cutthroats," I offered.

"Well, I think we should at least go out and look for her," Sam said again. "We could just drive around."

"Where? Spring City?" Peter said. "Holiday? Hartville?"

"How long do they make you wait until you can report somebody missing?" I asked.

"More than forty-five minutes," Holly said. "I don't think there's a lot you can do here but wait."

"This is my fault," Alicia's father said. "I've been so wrapped up in myself—"

Holly was just starting to make a conciliatory noise when the front door flew open.

Sam

And here is Alicia, bawling her head off.

At the same time, we hear somebody peeling out. Peter and I practically jam each other in the doorway, trying to get out there before the jerks get away.

Nikki

Alicia was sobbing. She was totally messed up—her clothes all twisted and grass-stained and her hair matted with old wet leaves.

As she came lunging inside, her dad yelled her name. She jumped a mile, screaming a little. Then she saw us all, and she collapsed against the wall, crying her heart out.

"What happened?" her father was roaring. "What did they do to you?"

Sam

The car goes screaming down the street. Peter takes off running down the walk. I'm right behind him. He gets to his car, and he's in it. I'm saying, "I'm coming," and he says, "No. This is mine." So he takes off after them alone, which is really stupid considering who he is chasing.

I think about following him. But I'm in my mother's car, and it's too late now, anyway. They are all way gone, and the street is quiet.

Not a lot left for me to do outside.

Unfortunately.

So I have to go back inside where Alicia is still wailing.

Nikki

Holly's face had gone white, and I was wringing my hands. I didn't know what to do. And I was scared.

"Bring her in here," Holly said finally, putting her hand on Alicia's father's shoulder. And to me, "Go see if you can find a blanket. *Go.*" So I tore upstairs and I found a quilt on the foot of one of the beds.

By the time I got back down, Alicia was propped up in one corner of the couch. There was a bruise on her cheek—or maybe it was dirt. Holly took the quilt from me and put it over Alicia, tucking it in all around. The sobbing had given way to a kind of whimpering, a sound I'd never heard Alicia make.

The front door opened again, and Sam came in. "They took off," he said.

"Where's Peter?" I asked him.

"He went after them," Sam said. "But they were already halfway across town." He looked at me and lowered his voice. "So, what happened?" All I could do was shake my head.

"What did he do?" her father kept asking.

"Go and get me a washcloth," Holly said to him, gently but firmly. "Warm water. Warm, not hot." I didn't think he would obey her, but he did.

Sam

So, in all the mayhem, this perfect stranger takes over. From the way Alicia's dad is treating her, he must pretty well think she's something. She's okay looking, too. He's done all right for himself, considering.

She reminds me more of my mom than Alicia's mom. I mean, I never heard Alicia's mother order Alicia's dad around the way this woman does.

Nikki

"Alicia," Holly said, pushing the matted hair off Alicia's forehead. "I'm Holly. I'm an old friend of your dad's." Alicia looked at her. "If you feel like you need anything, just say it," Holly told her. For a second, I was afraid of what Alicia might say, the way she was looking. But then she just shook her head.

Her father came back in with the washcloth, dripping all over the rug. "I'm going to call the police," he announced.

Then Alicia came to life. "No," she said. "Don't."

But he was headed for the phone.

She wailed, "Don't, Daddy. He didn't do anything."

"What do you mean? Look at you," he shouted.

"Greg," Holly said sharply.

"Well, look at her," he hollered.

"And yelling at her is going to help?" Holly said. She turned back to Alicia. "You want to tell us what happened then, honey?" she said. "That's the choice here—either you have to tell us exactly what happened, or we'll have to call the police. You'll have to tell them, anyway."

Alicia shook her head and started to sob again.

"That does it," her father said.

"No," Alicia roared. "They didn't *do* anything. They just—" She stopped and put her hand over her eyes.

"What, baby?" Holly asked gently, carefully putting the hair back.

"They said," Alicia said, spitting the words out very bitterly, "that if I was going to go with them, I had to be initiated. And then they drove to this park, and they pulled me out of the car—they just pulled me—and they were all laughing. And there were girls there, too, like that Janice Elton and that Alicia. . . . " She paused, her teeth clamped shut.

"And?" Holly prompted.

When Alicia spoke again, she had lowered her voice. She spoke carefully, maturely. "It was just a big joke. They threw me down on the ground, and one of them—" Then she balled up her fists and screamed through her teeth; I had never seen her like this.

"What?" her father demanded. "What?"

"Kissed me. He kissed me. Just grossly. Just—" She screwed up her face like she was going to spit. "And he was saying *things*. And I bit him, and they were all crowded around, and they were all saying these *things* and laughing, and I *hate* them and I want to *kill* them." She was screaming this with her teeth clenched. Her face had gone deep red.

"Then what?" her father asked, like he was about an inch from shaking it out of her.

"Then Morgan pulled the guy off of me. Morgan just stood there looking down at me, and he took me by the arm and jerked me up off the ground. And he said, 'Initiation failed.' And he *marched* me across the grass and pushed me into the car, and he made one of the girls drive me home."

"Get her some water," Holly told Sam.

"And all the way home," Alicia said, hiccupping now, "that girl just kept saying these things. These *things* . . ."

Sam brought her the water, and when she took it, her hands were shaking so badly, the water sloshed all over. Holly took it away from her and helped her drink it.

"Then I came home," she said, and started to cry. Normal crying.

Sam

I have to give Weiss some credit: he stopped them before they got too carried away. I don't think Alicia will be following him around with those earth-mother eyes of hers anymore. She's so delicate. This was a brutal thing for anybody to do. But it could have been so much worse.

Nikki

The adults were talking, over by the stairs.

I sat down on the floor next to the couch and put my hand on Alicia's arm. "Is that really all?" I asked, looking her in the eye.

She nodded. "Why did they have to do that?" she whispered. "And why did they laugh?"

"I don't know," I said. "I don't know. They're jerks. Stupid jerks."

"We should go," Sam said, standing behind me.

"No," Alicia said. "I don't want you to go."

"No," Holly said, coming back into the room. "We need to do something. We need to put something else into her head." Alicia was shivering. "Could you eat some pie and ice cream?" Holly asked. Alicia shook her head. "But I bet you could, huh?" Holly said to Sam. He shrugged, but he looked interested. "Okay, then," Holly said, and went into the kitchen. I got up and sat down on the couch where Holly had been.

"You want me to find them and kill them?" Sam asked.

Alicia looked up at him and laughed. It sounded painful. "No," she said bitterly. "They're already dead." She pressed on a temple. "I have a headache," she said.

"Do we need a doctor?" her father asked from the doorway.

"No injury," Alicia said. "Just humiliation."

"Disappointment," I added.

"Yeah," she said, her face collapsing again.

"Pie," Holly said, handing a plate to Sam. "You two," she said to Alicia's dad and me, "come get your own."

"I still want to call the police," her father said.

But Alicia shook her head. "What would you say? I don't even know which one kissed me. It'd be—I just want to forget it. Nobody really did anything. It was just a mean joke."

"I'm going to call them," he said, and he left the room again.

Holly just rolled her eyes.

Sam

Alicia's dad is calling the police. Nothing will come of it.

I think it would be better for everybody if it just ends here.

The pie is not bad. I have to say, it's good to eat again.

Nikki

"How about this?" Sam asked, holding up *What's Up, Doc?* "Make you laugh," he said, doing Groucho eyebrows.

We sat down with the pie and watched the movie. Holly put Alicia on the floor with her back against the couch so Holly could comb the leaves out of her hair.

After a while, a policeman came by to take the complaint. Alicia wouldn't give any names. Her father gave Morgan's, but Alicia told the policeman he hadn't done anything but save her, so I don't think they'll be doing much about it.

"You know," I told Alicia as her dad walked the policeman out, "I had a talk with Peter tonight. I really think you ought to forgive him, Alicia. You probably didn't notice, but he went after those guys tonight, all by himself. He was defending your honor."

She didn't say anything. But I could tell she was thinking.

The movie was almost over when the phone rang. Alicia's dad got up to answer it. Holly started picking up the pie plates.

Alicia's father came back in, rubbing the back of his neck. "That was Peter," he said. He looked at Sam. "You want to come with me?"

"Sure," Sam said. "Where're we going?"

"He was looking for those guys," I said.

Alicia's father nodded. "Well," he said wearily, "it seems that he found them."

#22

Nikki

Poor Peter. They took his car, and they might even have broken his nose. Whatever, he's going to have a classic set of shiners. At least the police have something they can do now; I only hope they find the car in one piece.

The upshot of this is: Peter is now a hero. A wounded one.

Alicia is overwhelmed by his undying devotion. "But he can't stay alone at his house," she cried pitifully. "He's hurt."

Fortunately for us all, Peter has a grandmother who is more than glad to put him up for a few days. If I were Peter, I wouldn't want to stay alone in that big house of his, not after a night like this.

Well. I suppose all's well that ends well. And really, this has not been such a bad ending. Tonight I saw Alicia furious, her father happy, and I heard Sam laugh.

I'd say things are looking up.

Alicia

The worst thing about this is going to be dealing with the fear. I don't want to go back to school on Monday. I don't even want to go out of the house, not ever again. I suppose I will have to go to church. And that should be okay. My dad will be with me. And Ann. I think Holly might be coming, too. I hope the nightmares go away very soon. And the flashbacks.

I don't know exactly how I should feel about this, but I realized last night, I liked having Holly around. Is that disloyal? Probably.

I'm too tired to worry about it. I was so angry last night. I'm still angry. Outraged. Furious. Terrified. At least it took my mind off my family for a few minutes.

Tonight, I am going to step out of my life for a little while. Holly is coming over again, and Dad is going to buy fried chicken, and Peter is going to come, too. They found his car today. It was a little trashed. And it was all the way in Hartville. Sam took him to pick it up.

We're going to play Scrabble and watch another movie and eat ice cream. I know some people can't appreciate an evening like that. But it sounds like heaven to me.

Sam

It is Saturday. I am cleaning out the front planters. I also have to climb up and clean the old leaf slime out of the rain gutters. When the mail finally comes, there is a letter for me.

I sit down on the rock wall of the now very empty planter. I turn the letter over in my hands. I don't know the address, but it is somewhere in this town.

I open the envelope, suddenly a little nervous about what might be in there.

"Hey, Boy Scout," it starts. I take a deep breath and look out over the street. It is a minute before I am brave enough to read the rest.

So, I'm in this place. It isn't too bad. It's this big old house, and there are about eight other girls here. These two girls in my room keep [whining] about having no privacy, but I have to laugh. They don't know how good they've got it. I can stay here until June, when I'll be an emancipated adult, so I can be on my own. These people say maybe the state will help for a while until I can get on my feet. But that won't be long. The people at Jon's place want me to work there as a staff assistant, and the head of the place wants me to come and live with her family until I can figure out what I want to do. It's just her and her daughter, so there's room, and she's always been very cool. My grades are good enough for college. So it looks like I have a future, anyway.

It also looks like they're going to haul Bradley's little [behind] into court over everything. That should be fun.

I am still really [mad] about what you did. I've come off it a little bit. Like, I'm no longer imagining ways I want you to die. I appreciate it that you went out to see Jon when I was messed up. But I still can't believe you betrayed me like that. And I still can't understand what you want. But frankly, I don't really want to know anymore. I don't know when I will cool down enough to forgive you, or if I ever will. But I wanted you to know that I am safer now, and that things are not exactly terrible for me.

[Very rude phrase]
Tia

A little while later, Nikki comes over. It's warm today, and the ground is pretty much dried out. So we just sit outside on the grass with the sun coming down on our faces. We stay there a long time, letting it get inside of us. And amazingly, nobody talks. When I finally open my eyes, I see the light shining on Nikki's head. It turns her hair all these colors. I never knew you could have green in your hair, but there are these little flashes of green and red and gold in there.

Nikki and I have been friends a long, long time. Her biggest fault is that she talks so much. Not that she's not interesting; it's just hard on my brain to have to process so much at once. But now I'm sitting out here, starting to wind down a little, and when she finally starts in again, her talk is background music. Like, I'm just here and she's just here, and it feels nice. Normal and good.

I look at her. I realize that it's nice, looking at her face, at the way her eyes get into what she's saying. I watch the way she wipes the grass off her palms. I take a deep breath, and suddenly my familiar life drops over me like an old quilt.

I have been thinking and thinking about all of this. I don't know how many Tia's there are in the world. The idea terrifies me. At my best, I couldn't save one of them.

Maybe I did her some good. I hope so. But Ms. Hyde is right; I can't live Tia's life for her, or Jon's or Alicia's, and I can't beat myself up over it. What good would that do? You get the life you get. You have to work with that. Be as useful and kind as you possibly can. And then try harder. That's the best you can do.

When I think this, I don't feel so bad. We talk about that kind of thing a little, Nikki and I. It feels good to talk to somebody who understands what I want. I can't tell her specifics about Tia. I could if it were only my story, but it's not.

I am thinking about taking Nikki with me when I visit Jon on Monday. "What?" she says, because now I am laughing. I am trying to imagine this, wondering if she will freak as badly as I did that first time. Then it occurs to me that Tia would be seriously outraged if she finds out I brought Nikki there. For some reason, that makes me laugh even more.

"You're nice." Nikki sniffs. Then she slugs me one. Suddenly, for the first time in a very long time, I feel completely happy.

I think it would do both Tia and Nikki some good to know each other. In some ways, I think they are a little alike. But maybe I'm wrong about that. Who knows what anybody is really like?

I look across the street. Matt Holyoak is headed into his house with a garment bag. Right then, I remember that tonight's the prom. I look at Nikki. Suddenly, I want to go. Suddenly, I want to buy a flower and go eat and dance and laugh with her.

When I ask, she doesn't say anything too rude.

Nikki

"Tonight? With you?" I asked, fluttering my eyelashes.

"Tonight. With me," he answered, fluttering his eyelashes.

"Sure," I said. "But I want a flower. And I want dinner."

He nodded.

"And you have"—I looked at my watch—"three hours to find a tux. And I have to find a dress." I poked him in the shoulder. "And you have to dance."

He looked pained. "I suppose I have to pay, too," he said.

I nodded, smiling very sweetly. "And don't forget pictures."

He took a deep breath with his eyes closed. "Okay," he said. He got up off the grass and held a hand out to me.

"But you have to drive," he told me.

"Why?" I asked him. "Where's the Jeep?"

He pointed toward the garage. "Can't drive it till next week," he said.

"Why?" I asked him. "Did you wreck it?"

"Nope," he said, giving my very sweet smile right back to me. "I forgot to take out the trash."